MW01134333

DOWN & DIRTY: LINC

Dirty Angels MC, Book 9

JEANNE ST. JAMES

Editor: Proofreading by the Page
Cover Art: Susan Garwood of Wicked Women Designs
Beta Readers: Author Whitley Cox, Krisztina Hollo, Andi Babcock and Sharon Abrams

www.jeannestjames.com

Sign up for my newsletter for insider information, author news, and new releases:
www.jeannestjames.com/newslettersignup

Warning: This book contains sexually explicit scenes and adult language and may be considered offensive to some readers. This book is for sale to adults ONLY, as defined by the laws of the country in which you made your purchase. Please store your files wisely, where they cannot be accessed by under-aged readers.

DISCLAIMER: Please do not try any new sexual practice without the guidance of an experienced practitioner. The author will not be responsible for any loss, harm, injury or death resulting from use of the information contained in this book.

Keep an eye on her website at http://www.jeannestjames.com/or sign up for her newsletter to learn about her upcoming releases: http://www.jeannestjames.com/newslettersignup

Down & Dirty 'til Dead

CHAPTER ONE

"I'm pregnant."

Behind the bar, Linc turned slowly to look at Jayde. She'd been standing there for about ten minutes and he'd ignored her every second of those minutes. For a good fucking reason, too.

He didn't want anything to do with her.

No fucking way.

She was dangerous. And no matter how much he'd wanted to touch her, smell her, taste her, he knew he would be taking his life in his own hands by doing so.

"Congrats," he muttered through clenched teeth, keeping his face neutral and trying to slow his racing heartbeat. He grabbed the nearest towel and began to scrub at the shellacked bar top, even though it was already clean.

Thank fuck it wasn't him who got snagged. Some other sucker was tied to her for the rest of his life. Stuck with dealing with her goddamn family.

"Same to you," she said softly.

His spine stiffened, his hand froze. He slowly lifted his head and met her blue eyes. The ones that always got him right in the gut. In the dick, too. "Whataya mean?"

"It's yours."

He shook his head. He must not have heard her right. "No."

"Yes, Linc."

Linc let his gaze slide through The Iron Horse Roadhouse. Though it wasn't busy, he wanted to make sure no one else had heard her. Especially one of the fucking brothers.

He wasn't in the mood to get his ass thumped tonight. Or any night. Even though he was good with his fists and Slade had been teaching him better boxing techniques, he didn't want to get down and dirty with any of his club brothers.

He moved closer to her, the wide polished wood bar the only thing separating the two of them, and whispered, "How?"

She arched a dark brow at him. "Really? Do I need to teach you about the birds and the bees? You seem to have that all figured out. Hence... our predicament."

He planted his palms on the bar and leaned in close. So close that he could see every shade of blue in her eyes. "Jayde, this shit ain't fuckin' funny."

She lifted one shoulder. "It's definitely not a joke. It's true."

He blew out a shaky breath, straightened, and rubbed the back of his hand across his mouth, then wrapped his fingers around the back of his neck, squeezing tightly. "Can't be. Only did it once. Fuckin' assured me you were on the pill."

"If you haven't heard, once can be enough. And... And the pill isn't one hundred percent effective."

Holy fuck.

Linc closed his eyes and saw his life flash before them. Her family consisted of two fucking cops and the DAMC president.

He was fucked. So goddamned fucked.

He had a feeling he'd end up in jail on some trumped-up charges, shot with a service weapon, or mysteriously disappearing by one of Diesel's "Shadows."

He'd knocked up Sergeant Mitchell Jamison's baby girl. And the baby sister of not only Corporal Axel Jamison, but Zak Jamison, the Dirty Angels MC president.

For fuck's sake, this couldn't be happening.

He groaned, his stomach a hollow pit. "Please tell me this is a fuckin' joke, Jayde."

Why the hell did she look so calm? Shouldn't she be upset? Freaking out?

Jayde shook her head, her long dark brown hair brushing over her shoulders. He had sunk his teeth into the smooth, ivory flesh of one of those that night.

"It's not. Sorry you're so disappointed."

His head jerked back. "What the fuck? And you're not?"

She gave him a small smile and dropped her hand to her belly, which was still as flat as ever.

Of fucking course, it would be. He'd finally given in to her only two months ago. Despite his resistance and every attempt at keeping a level head, she had worn him down until the night of Kiki and Hawk's wedding...

Shit.

She had got to him when he was buzzing on whiskey. When his walls were down. When she was wearing a sexy as fuck red low-cut dress that showed off her tits, clung to her hips, and swirled around her luscious thighs. When he couldn't fight what he wanted any longer.

A moment of weakness... could turn out to be the biggest mistake of his life.

Jester, the newest patched member, moved down the bar with a shot of something in his tattooed hand for one of the customers. As he slid behind Linc, he greeted, "Hey, Jayde. Lookin' good, babe."

Linc's spine snapped straight.

Jayde gave Jester a small smile. "Hey, Jester."

Jester hesitated, his smile widening. "Watcha doin' hangin' out here? Gonna stay for a bit?"

With a growl, Linc grabbed the shot glass out of the younger brother's hand and downed it before slapping it onto the bar.

"Hey!" Jester yelled. "That was for the fuckin' guy on the end."

"Don't give a shit. Get him another. Watch the bar. Me and Jayde need to talk."

Jester's gaze slid from Linc to Jayde and back to Linc. "'Bout what?"

"If I wanted you to fuckin' know, I'd talk to her right fuckin' here. Watch the damn bar." With that, he pushed past Jester and rounded the end of the long bar. When he got to her, he grabbed her elbow tightly and pulled her off the stool. "Let's go."

She blinked her baby blues up at him. "Where are we going?"

Linc stilled and blew out a breath. That was a good question. He couldn't take her into church. There'd be too many curious eyes and ears in there. He couldn't take her up to his room because that would be like asking for a fucking ass whooping. And the kitchen was full of employees doing their thing right now.

Shit.

"Your car out front?" he finally asked.

"Yes. Why?"

He pulled her toward the front entrance. Good thing Hawk had been in earlier in the evening to check on the bar. Now he was home with his wife, Kiki, and newborn where he planted his ass almost every night lately. Otherwise, the big man might have stepped in, thinking their president's little sister needed protecting.

He steered her out the door and through the dark lot, looking for her Camaro. The one her *father* bought for her. The father who was going to string him up by his fucking nuts.

He finally spotted the bright yellow Chevy and as soon as she dug the remote from her purse, he snagged it from her fingers and popped the locks. He stopped at the passenger side door, swung it open and shoved her gently toward it, indicating she was riding shotgun.

"Why—"

He cut her off. "Get in."

"But—"

"Just get in. No lip, woman."

With a loud, exaggerated sigh, she slid into the passenger seat.

He shut the door and, as he moved around to the driver's side, shrugged out of his cut and quickly turned it inside out before slipping it back on over his Harley tee. He yanked the door open and climbed in.

Or tried to, since he was practically eating the steering wheel. *What the fuck.*

He jabbed the power button and the seat moved back until he could breathe. Hitting the ignition, the car roared to life.

The car was fucking sweet.

So was Jayde.

But he never should've gotten in either one of them.

He could feel her eyes burning a hole into the side of his head.

"I thought we were going to talk?"

He unlocked his jaw. "If you fuckin' think I'm sitting at The Iron Horse in *your* car, you're fuckin' crazy, woman. Don't need anyone seeing us in a car together. Gonna drive somewhere safe. And dark. Hopefully your fuckin' father or brother ain't on patrol so they can rip me outta the car and taze my ass before using me for target practice."

"They won't—"

"Right," he grunted. Even though it was only spring, he turned the A/C on full blast. For some reason, he had fucking sweat beading on his forehead. After shoving the car into drive, he stabbed the gas pedal to get them the hell out of dodge. "Stupid you showing up at the bar. Just stupid, Jayde."

"You needed to know."

He hardly heard her answer over the thumping of his heart in his ears. With a grunt, he shook his head. "You don't tell me that kind of shit in public. In the club's bar, for fuck's sake. Coulda texted me and I'da met you somewhere."

"You'd never agree to meet me anywhere. You don't even respond to my texts anymore."

He could hear it in her voice. The thickness, the sadness. He closed his eyes for a second and steeled himself against it. "Reason for it."

"Apparently," she answered softly. "You don't want me."

No. That wasn't the fucking reason. Linc wanted her. Fuck, he wanted her like a drug addict wanted their next fix. From the first time he saw her crossing the common area at church when he was a prospect. Her hips had rocked and rolled across the room as she came to see Z, who was fresh out of prison. Jayde hadn't seen her brother in ten years, the whole time Zak spent locked up. But she had gone against her father's wishes and showed up to welcome her brother home anyway.

He knew right then and there she was a gutsy spitfire. He could see it in her flashing blue eyes. Could see it in her walk. In her attitude. But he only watched her over the years, knowing she was *one-hundred-fucking-percent* off-limits. It would be bad enough to go against his president's wishes, but her cop father and brother?

Oh. Fuck. No.

It was bad enough that Mitch Jamison hated the fact that Z was a part of the MC. And he certainly wasn't happy that his youngest son was shacking up with Bella, a DAMC born and bred biker chick.

Mitch wanted nothing to do with the club that his own father, Bear, had started. Not one damn thing. And now a biker may have knocked up his daughter? His little girl?

Linc tucked a hand in between his legs, holding onto his balls. He had a feeling he'd be losing them soon.

He pulled the Camaro into a dark, empty parking lot that was tucked behind a closed business. They couldn't be seen from the road and hopefully the cops wouldn't be swinging through anytime soon.

He shoved the shifter into park, rolled the windows down, shut the Chevy off and sucked warm night air through his nostrils. He needed to tamp down the urge to puke.

He twisted in his seat and stared at the woman in the shadows of the car.

"Want you, Jayde. Want you so fuckin' bad. But also like breathing." He lifted a palm to stop her when she turned toward him with her mouth open. "Ain't here to talk about that. Need to know how you know it's mine? How do I know you ain't pawning some other fucker's kid off on me?"

Even in the limited light, it was obvious her jaw dropped open, and her eyes narrowed.

He ignored her outrage. "Can't tell me I was the only one."

She hadn't been a virgin when they hooked up. Hell, the fucking woman had gone off to college. No woman survived college without at least getting laid once, right?

His jaw tightened at the thought of some college boy laying between her soft thighs, dipping his dick into her. Probably just trying to get himself off and leaving Jayde in the dust.

He hadn't. Fuck no. He'd made sure she came at least three times before he popped a nut. Unfortunately, he popped it inside her and hadn't had a wrap with him. But then, they were at a DAMC wedding and he wasn't planning on getting laid that night. It wasn't like there was going to be any available strange at the celebration.

She also said that night she was on the pill. But at The Iron Horse she stated it wasn't always effective. Had she lied about being on the pill at all?

No matter what, he had only expected to sit, drink and watch Jayde from a distance as she danced with the club sisters. Then he planned on going back to his room at church and whacking off at least once to that memory.

But when she continued to tease him from across the room and then again in a dark, hidden spot outside the large tent...

When she got up on her tiptoes and took his mouth, shoved her tongue inside, then ground her belly against his hard dick as a sexy moan bubbled up her throat...

There was only so much a man could take.

Especially since she had been the fodder for his daily whack-offs for years.

Finally, when he got to sink into her soft, wet heat...

Fuck.

And that was after he got to taste her sweet, silky honey. Something he hadn't forgotten to this day.

He closed his eyes and drew his tongue over his bottom lip in remembrance. The oxygen left his lungs and his dick twitched in his jeans.

Fuck.

When she whispered, "Linc," on a shaky breath and touched his thigh, he stiffened, and his eyes popped open.

He brushed her hand off. Her touching him was going to make it harder for him to keep his head on straight. "Who knows?"

She dropped her hand back into her lap with her other one and stared out of the windshield. "No one yet. I wanted you to be the first to know."

Well, thank fuck for small miracles. There may be a way out of this mess yet. He steeled himself for what he said next, "Ain't telling nobody. Getting rid of it."

She gasped, and her head spun in his direction. "No. I... No. No, Linc."

He shook his head. "Gotta, Jayde. Got your life ahead of you, this will fuck up your plans of finishing law school and shit. You can't. We can't."

The woman wanted to finish law school. To pass the bar and join Kiki's firm as a partner instead of just an assistant. This would fuck everything up. She had big dreams. She needed to follow them. She didn't need to be tied down with a kid.

"I could still finish school," she whispered.

"How? Law school is fuckin' expensive. How are you gonna pay for that if your daddy don't do it for you?"

"I've been saving... Kiki..."

He shook his head. "You'll be disowned, Jayde. Your father... Hell, your brothers..." He swallowed hard and tried a different approach. "Being a dad ain't for me."

"How do you know? Look at Diesel."

"Jewel is D's ol' lady."

"So? You think that makes a difference?"

"Fuck yeah, it does!" he yelled. He squeezed his eyes shut for a second, then responded more calmly with, "Yeah, it does."

"Violet wasn't planned."

No shit. No one forgot the shocker of D going down like a tree in the middle of a Redwood forest. "But they got a connection. They were together before she got knocked up."

"And we can be together after."

He shook his head. "No. I live above church. You're still living with mommy and daddy, for fuck's sake!"

"We'll get a place."

"No."

"Linc."

No. No. No. He didn't want to be the reason she fucked up her whole life. Saddled her with a kid. Dashed her dreams of becoming a lawyer. Made things rough between her and her family.

Just fuck no.

She would eventually regret it and come to hate him.

He couldn't live with that.

She was smart. She should know this would screw up her plans for her future.

She was college educated, had career goals. Why the hell would she even want to have a kid with a biker like him?

He needed for her to see the sense in what he was saying.

"No, Jayde. Fuck no. This ain't right. Don't wanna fuckin' kid and don't want one with you."

CHAPTER TWO

J ayde lost her breath at his words. Her stomach twisted into a knot.

Don't wanna fuckin' kid and don't want one with you.

She was stupid. Totally fucking stupid. She should've known that he wasn't going to jump up and down with joy, then drop to one knee and propose after expressing his deep love for her.

What the hell had she been thinking?

He was right. This was a complete disaster. Even so, she hadn't expected him to say that she should terminate the pregnancy. That had caught her completely off guard.

It seemed as though all the women in the club were either pregnant or just had babies. She had to admit, baby fever had swept through her. Though, she didn't plan this. Maybe he thought she had.

Maybe he thought she was trying to trap him.

She wasn't.

Yes, she'd been attracted to him from the first day she spotted him across the common room at church. He'd been a prospect everyone called Abe at the time. He'd been playing pool and his green eyes had followed her intently as she crossed the room on her way to see her brother, who had just been released from prison.

When Z walked her back out to her car, Linc had watched her every move then, too. She couldn't ignore his heated gaze and it had made butterflies flutter in her stomach. And even lower.

Even though she'd been ordered to stay away from church, to stay away from the DAMC, to stay away from bikers in general by her father, she'd snuck over to the clubhouse time and time again. Just to see Linc.

To watch him. To talk to him. To be near him.

To breathe his scent. To hear his voice.

It gave her something to hold onto when she was in her room, in the dark, alone at night.

He'd been interested, too. At least until that fateful day the Warriors had shot up The Iron Horse during the club's Christmas party. Linc had covered her with his own body, shielded her from the bullets and the flying shrapnel. Risked his life for her.

Because of that, she swore she fell in love with him a little bit that night. Then her father showed up and caught them together. Not doing anything except talking, but it was enough for him to go off on Linc, threaten to kill him if the man ever touched his daughter.

It didn't matter to her father that Jayde had been in her mid-twenties at the time. An adult and certainly not a virgin. She was still her father's "little girl." Probably always would be.

Their father made sure his kids weren't part of the DAMC and remained on the outskirts. Her father had dragged himself away from the club a long time ago. He'd decided to take a different path, and not follow in his own father's footsteps. Especially after her grandfather, one of the founders of the DAMC, was killed by a rival MC.

Mitch Jamison had walked away and never looked back. He went to the police academy and stayed on the straight and narrow. Unlike his brother, Rocky, who, after dishing out retribution for Bear being killed, ended up in SCI Greene for multiple counts of murder.

Her father always said that he followed the light instead of falling into the darkness.

Mitch dragged her older brother Axel along with him toward that light, encouraging him to become a cop, too. He did. Both of them loved their jobs and did them well.

Then there was Zak...

Her oldest brother had patched into the club as soon as he could, despite their father's disapproval. Became DAMC president at an unheard of early age, then...

Then he spent ten years in prison for a crime he didn't commit. For something he was set up for.

Now he was back at the head of the table and their father was livid about it. While Z worked hard to keep the club above water, both financially and legally, murder and chaos still managed to seep in. There always seemed to be cracks that her brother couldn't plug. Rivals he couldn't rid them of.

Like the Shadow Warriors.

Time and time again, that outlaw nomad MC had wreaked havoc on the DAMC. They'd been a threat for decades.

So Linc was right, her father was going to blow a gasket because she was reckless and got knocked up by a biker whom he detested.

Maybe this wasn't the best time for her to bring a child into their lives. But was there ever a perfect time?

Her hand pressed against her stomach as she dropped her head, letting her long hair curtain her face to hide the hot, hopeless tears that spilled down her cheeks.

A life had been created inside of her. A combination of two souls. A gift that Bella could only wish she could provide Jayde's brother, Axel. And here Linc wanted her to get rid of something that someone else, like Bella, would take in a second. A gift she would cherish.

Maybe Bella and Axel could adopt the baby, raise the child as theirs if Linc didn't want it.

Or Jayde could just raise the baby herself. Her mother would help, but her father would most likely make her life unbearable.

Eventually he might come around, since he didn't have any grand-children yet besides Zeke. Though, stubbornly, he refused to give in and let Zak bring his son over to the house. Not that Z wanted to. Their mom even had to go behind her dad's back to see her firstborn grandson.

Axel and Bella would never be able to provide grandchildren. Unless they decided to adopt. So one would think her father would appreciate the only grandchild he had.

Maybe her father would shut out her child like he did with Baby Z. He'd definitely kick her out of the house. She'd end up on her own, struggling to make it and provide for her own child.

Linc was right. She'd never be able to return to law school this fall if she had this baby. She'd never even lived on her own. The only time she'd lived away from her parents was during her first four years of college, which *they* paid for.

Her father even bought her a fucking car!

What the hell was she thinking? She was now twenty-eight years old and ended up being one of those adult children that still lived with their parents and relied on them for *everything*!

She was no better than one of those basement dwellers, who lived in their childhood home, that her and her friends made fun of on dating apps.

She was such a loser.

And now the only man she truly wanted to be with was pissed.

Her body hiccuped as a sob ripped through her.

Holy shit! She was going to ugly cry in the car sitting next to Linc. Her mascara was going to run, her eyes and nose were going to get red and puffy, and...

A large hand grabbed her chin, lifted her face and turned it toward him.

"Sorry, baby. Didn't mean to make you fuckin' cry. Just shocked the shit outta me."

She sniffled, keeping her eyes tipped downward. "No, I'm sorry. It's all my fault."

"Fuckin' Jayde. Ain't all your fault. I fucked up by not being prepared."

"I pressured you. I—"

"Woman," he said softly, stroking a thumb over her cheek, cutting through the stream of tears. "Didn't do anything I didn't wanna do. And I wanted to do you."

And I wanted to do you.

"It was just sex," she stated flatly, staring at the center console.

"Yeah."

"And now this."

"Yeah. Gonna deal with it."

Right. Deal with it. A few hundred dollars later their "problem" would be solved.

The ache in her chest increased and she rubbed at it. He captured her hand and dragged it into his lap, squeezing it.

"Jayde, want you, baby, I do. But this shit… This ain't the way to go about it. When you aren't under your father's thumb, we can revisit it. Until then…"

"Until then, you want to get rid of the evidence of our mistake." The disappointment of this decision—one she hadn't expected to come from his mouth when she had showed up at The Iron Horse—washed through her. It made her heart thump in her chest and the tears fall even faster.

"Jayde, baby. Only want what's best for you," he whispered.

Her eyes flicked up to his face. He feared her family. Maybe rightly so. He only wanted what was "best" for *her*. Sure he did.

"Bullshit," she bit off. "Bullshit, Linc. You want what's best for you."

"Got no future, Jayde. You do. Don't got a college degree, a big career planned. Know what I got? This fuckin' club. My sled. A room above church. That's it. I'm a fuckin' bartender in a fuckin' biker bar. Can't offer you anything. Got shit."

"You have me. And now this baby."

Linc shook his head. "Been dancing 'round each other for years. Finally fucked once. That shit don't make a relationship, Jayde. It fuckin' don't. Don't make good parents, either. Trust me, I've seen it with other folks."

She lifted her head and brushed away the hair that clung to her damp cheeks. She studied him through blurry eyes. He was right again, damn it. She didn't know much about him besides his time in the club. She had no idea where he came from or anything about his family.

He knew everything about hers.

She could understand why this news would scare the shit out of him. All three male Jamisons—her father and her two brothers—would want to kill him. They would see it as defiling their little sister and daughter. They wouldn't understand that she had wanted to be with Linc as much as he'd wanted to be with her that night. They would lay the blame solely at Linc's feet.

Jayde would be the "poor innocent girl" that Linc took advantage of. That wouldn't be fair to him.

She knew he'd been buzzing the night of Hawk and Kiki's wedding reception. She had taken advantage of *him* while he was weak. Not the other way around.

She would need to make sure her father and brothers knew that. She needed to make that very clear.

She had mistakenly thought once he had a taste of her, he wouldn't be able to resist her anymore. He was wrong on one thing. They hadn't been *dancing 'round each other*. No. He'd been keeping her at arm's length for a while.

But they'd hooked up almost two months ago and since then, nothing. Not one text, one call, nothing. She gave. He took. And then he didn't look back.

"Jayde," he murmured, and she tried to focus on his face in the limited light. Though she couldn't see him clearly, she knew what he looked like only all too well. His tightly trimmed hair, the color of maple syrup, his intense moss green eyes. His strong jaw. His numerous tattoos, which seemed to have exploded in number once he patched in about three years ago. He'd let Crow do what Crow did best. Linc had given the tattoo artist free rein to practice on him. So now Linc had two full sleeves and the night of Hawk and Kiki's wedding Jayde saw what was hidden under that T-shirt. Solid tats. Over his chest and stomach. His back sported the colors of loyalty and family—the DAMC rockers and center patch—like all the rest of the fully-patched brothers had. His legs—when she had seen them two months ago—made up of long and lean muscle were almost tattoo-free except for the barbed wire tat that circled one ankle.

"Baby," he murmured again, stroking his thumb gently over her cheek.

She had stopped crying because tears weren't going to help their situation.

"If you weren't who you are, then shit would be different. But you are, and it ain't. It's never gonna work."

"Because of my father and my brothers."

"Yeah, 'cause of them. Might not have a college degree but I'm not stupid."

"I know you aren't. Hawk always says you have a lot of smarts and have a good head on your shoulders. That you run The Iron Horse like it's your own and you manage it well."

Linc grunted.

"If it wasn't for you, he'd still be tied down with the bar and unable to spend more time with Kiki and the baby. Kiki's grateful for you, too."

"She say that?"

"Yes," Jayde whispered. "She said Hawk wants to rely on you more, especially since her firm is busy as hell and he needs to step up with Ashton." Kiki had just come back to the office after giving birth to their son Ash about a month ago and was finding it a struggle to leave the baby unless she left him in Hawk's care. Especially since the Warriors still existed.

Linc grunted in answer again.

She sniffled and smiled. He was so like the rest of his club brothers. He had fit in perfectly, even when he was only a prospect. There was never a doubt he'd become a DAMC brother. Not one.

He slid his thumb over her lips. "That's it, baby. Need to smile, not cry. Fuckin' beautiful when you smile."

"So are you," she whispered.

He shook his head. "Nothing beautiful about me."

"If there wasn't, you wouldn't have caught my eye."

Linc sighed, wrapped his fingers around the back of her neck, squeezed, then pulled her face to within inches of his. Even in the dark his gaze was intense, searching. "What're we gonna do, Jayde?" he asked in a rough whisper.

"Have a baby," she answered just as softly.

With that, she closed the small gap between their mouths, pressing hers to his. He didn't fight it. His only reaction at first was his fingers digging harder into the muscles of her neck.

His lips opened, and he took over, kissing her hard, tilting his head to tighten the connection, to make sure he could explore her whole mouth. Their tongues tangled, and he captured her moan before giving it back to her.

The fingers at her neck slipped into her hair and, grabbing a fistful, he yanked her head back and kissed her even harder, crushing her lips. Blindly, she reached for her seatbelt and unfastened it. She climbed to her knees on the seat without breaking the kiss, their tongues now sparring. His other hand dragged down the front of her throat, over her chest until he cupped her breast over her shirt. Then his fingers found her puckered nipple and twisted it through her clothing. She gasped, breaking the kiss, and tried to pull her head back, but he wouldn't let go of her hair.

"Fuckin' Jayde," he murmured against her lips. He snagged her bottom lip between his teeth and tugged gently before releasing it. "That fuckin' mouth. *Fuck.*" He shoved his face into her neck, his breathing coming rapidly as he scraped his teeth down her throat, along her pounding pulse.

Her breasts were so tender lately. One of the signs that had suggested she needed to pick up a pregnancy test at the drug store, in addition to the obvious one of her cycle being late.

She squeezed her eyes shut as she pictured the test stick in her hand and the panic that had bulldozed right over her when she saw those two lines. Two little blue lines that had paralyzed her for a few days. Until she let the reality of what those lines meant to her. To Linc. To her future.

A thought swirled around in her head and before she could stop it, it broke free. "I should've just sucked you off that night and we never would've had a problem."

He huffed, his warm breath moving her hair by her cheek, and put his lips to her ear. "Then I never woulda felt how hot, wet, sweet, and tight your fuckin' pussy was as it wrung my dick dry."

What he said was crude, but it still sent a bolt of lightning through her. A shock that landed in her core. It made her as wet as that night two months ago.

She had never reacted like that with any of the men—no, *boys*— she'd been with before. None of the guys she'd slept with in college had done half of what Linc had done for her during that single, fateful night. Not that there'd been a lot of guys. She had exactly two. She'd dated each of them for months before figuring out they were selfish pricks.

Linc had been the only man who'd ever brought her to an orgasm during sex. At least not a self-induced one, anyway.

He'd been the only one who made sure she lost her mind before he lost his.

She thought they'd made a solid connection that night...

That he cared as much about her as she did about him.

Her heart was pounding, her nipples painfully peaked, her pussy throbbed. She dropped her hand to his lap finding his hardness, his heat through his jeans. He wanted her. He couldn't deny it.

But, again, it could simply be for sex. She could just be a "hole to bust a nut into" like the guys said so easily and so often.

He snagged her hand where she'd been tracing her fingers over his length through the denim. He pulled it away, pressed his forehead to hers and panted, "Jayde, not in the car. Not here. You deserve better than that."

"Backseat," she suggested, her body humming with wanting him.

She didn't want to take the time to find somewhere else. She didn't want to wait.

"No."

"Yes, backseat. Just give me this."

"No, baby, you deserve better."

"Than what? Than you? Than fucking in the backseat of my car?" She winced at the high pitch of her own voice.

"Yeah, so much fuckin' better than that."

She shook her head. "And you don't?"

"Jayde," he murmured against her cheek.

"Linc, *please*, just fuck me. I want to feel something other than sadness, than fear, than the panic which has seeped into my bones for the past few days. Ever since I found out—"

"Don't got a wrap."

Jayde pulled back, her brows raised. "Really?"

Linc huffed another breath. "Yeah, that was fuckin' dumb."

Her lips twitched. "Yes. It was." She pulled away from him, flung open the passenger side door and climbed out into the warm late spring night. Hitting the power button, she moved the passenger seat as far forward as it could go, then stood outside the door stripping off her clothes one piece at a time as he watched her. She tossed each piece into the car and when she finally stood naked outside her Camaro, she ducked into the back. He still only stared at her, almost as if in a trance.

"Linc," she breathed, running her hands over her tender breasts. They felt heavy and full, her nipples peaked painfully.

She wanted his hands on her, not her own.

He shook his head. "Ain't smart, Jayde."

So? It wasn't smart. Not using a condom almost two months ago wasn't smart, either. They were paying for it now. But that didn't mean they couldn't enjoy each other tonight, before the rest of the world found out they fucked up. *If* they found out they fucked up. Linc had other ideas.

Right now, she just wanted to remind him how much they'd wanted each other for so long. Remind him how good it was between them weeks ago. That they could be good together for the rest of their lives.

If he wanted that.

She was open to it.

She knew it would be difficult for her and him. But Jayde looked up to Kiki. A brilliant, successful attorney who ended up with Hawk, the VP of the Dirty Angels. They came from two different worlds and they loved each other so deeply... Anyone who saw them together could see it, taste it, feel it. Their bond was unmistakable.

Kiki never looked down on Hawk for being a badass, tattooed biker. Not once. She loved him for who he was, how he was and never once asked him to change. She drew from his strength and Hawk drew from hers. They had built the perfect life with each other, even after tragedy.

Then she considered Bella and Axel. Her older brother a cop, practically a clone of their father, but he had found love and happiness with a born and bred biker chick. Did they have issues? Yes. Issues they couldn't overcome? Not yet. Hopefully never.

Linc and her could have that. They could take this mistake and build something from it. Something worthwhile.

He just needed to see that.

He just needed to see how much she wanted him. She didn't care that he was a biker. That shit ran through her veins. She was born with that in her blood, she had no idea if Linc had it in his. He could be first generation biker. Hell, his parents could be straight-laced CPAs for all she knew.

Didn't matter. He was now DAMC through and through. And to Jayde, that meant loyalty and family. As much as her father demanded that she stay away from the club, something always pulled at her when it came to the Angels. The deep rumble of the straight pipes, the shine of the polished chrome. The smell of whiskey and gasoline. The tattoos. The club colors. The motto: *Down & Dirty 'til Dead*. The fact that none of them acted like they gave a fuck, when deep down they really did.

Every single one of them was passionate about their ol' lady.

Once they found the right one, the woman that made everything about their life right, they hung on for dear life. They'd lay down their own lives for their woman. For their kids. Their club. Their family meant everything. Blood or not.

Jayde wanted that. And she wanted it with Linc.

So, she spread her knees, leaned back against the seat and let her fingers trail down her stomach to the apex of her thighs. One hand kneaded a breast, while the other strummed slowly through her damp folds. She circled one fingertip over her clit and her eyelids drooped heavily, her mouth parted, and puffs of breath escaped.

Linc still sat there in the driver's seat, almost frozen, most likely fighting what he wanted. What he craved. But even in the dim lighting, she could see his Adam's apple jump when his eyes dropped to the shadow at the V of her legs. He probably couldn't see what she was doing, but he certainly could imagine it.

A hoarse whisper escaped him, "Jayde."

"Am I going to have to do this all by myself?"

His cut and T-shirt were off in record time. Somehow, he squeezed his large body between the front seats and over the center console without breaking anything. By the time he landed chest-first on the back seat with a grunt, he had his jeans pushed down to his knees.

It was Jayde's turn to freeze as she watched him wiggle like a snake, twisting and turning, yanking off his boots and socks, and finally working his jeans off even though they ended up inside out and somehow landing on the dash.

There wasn't a lot of room in the back of that Camaro, but he huffed and puffed until he was totally naked and finally sitting on the seat next to her. Then all of a sudden, he grabbed her ankles and yanked. She squealed as she slid forward, almost cracking her head against the interior of the car. He propped one of her bare feet on the back of the passenger seat and the other on the edge of the back sill, then he dove...

Literally dove forward until his face was shoved between her thighs. Her cry filled the car as his mouth found her, working her heated, wet flesh with a skill that brought back memories from that late night a couple of months ago. She had been surprised he had brought her to orgasm with just his mouth last time. She wondered if he could do it again.

Her fingers dug into his scalp and held him close, not that he was going anywhere. His tongue flicked and circled her clit as her hips rose and fell slightly on the leather seat. Then he sucked and nibbled that sensitive nub, making her scream and shove his face tighter against her.

She swore he chuckled against her swollen flesh. But he didn't stop. Oh hell no, he didn't. He added two fingers and sucked and fucked her until her head fell back against the rear passenger window and her mouth opened, a long, loud wail escaping.

Her nails dug into his scalp. "I'm..."

His broad tongue lapped and licked.

"I'm..."

The tip of his tongue pressed and teased.

"I'm..."

His fingers curled inside her.

"I'm... *ooooh... fuuuuuck*..." Her hips shot up and her whole body convulsed, her thighs squeezing his head, but he didn't let up until the waves of her climax finished and her body went limp.

Then he pressed his cheek against her inner thigh and kissed her softly.

He was breathing as hard as she was, his warm breath brushing along her damp skin, tickling her now tender pussy which was still open for him, waiting for him to make the next move.

"Wish things could be different, Jayde."

No. She didn't need to hear that right now. That's not what she needed at that very moment.

She needed *him*, and she needed to forget everything but the two of them. Even if it was just for a brief time in her car. The rest of the world, their problems could stay outside of that safe bubble for the time being.

"We're not done," she murmured. When he gave her a sharp nod, she knew he had it all wrong. He thought she meant sex.

But she had meant so much more.

They weren't done. There was a reason they'd caught each other's eyes all those years ago. There was a reason Jayde had no one else since the day she spotted him across the room.

Because even though they had never gotten together, except for that single time, she knew in that moment when her eyes met his, that he was hers. He was put on this Earth for her. And she belonged to him.

Maybe this baby was meant to push them together, to strengthen what she suspected they could have, if only her family didn't stand in the way.

Maybe the baby would fill those deep fractures between her father, Axel and Zak. Linc was a good man, a loyal one, which was proven by his actions with the DAMC. Zak would come around easily. Her father and Axel, not so much.

She pushed all of that out of her head. She wanted this to be their time, hers and Linc's. No one else was invited.

Even though her legs still felt like jelly, she shifted enough until he needed to sit up and once he did, she moved to straddle his lap. His cock was hard and hot as it pushed against her belly. He was ready for her.

But she didn't want to rush it. She wanted them to take their time. Though, she doubted that would happen. The back of her Chevy was not an ideal place to be intimate, to draw out pleasures, to appreciate each other.

No, the back of the car wasn't for that. It was for quickies and getting off.

But they had nowhere else to go. She lived with her parents and he lived above church. And the last thing they needed was to get caught at the Shadow Valley Motor Inn.

She spread the fingers of both hands along the sides of his face and pulled him to her. "Kiss me," she breathed.

He did. Again, taking control, not even hesitating for a second.

His tongue swept through her mouth, his hands which had been at her waist, moved up slowly, his fingers brushed along her ribs, then the outer curves of her breasts. He broke the kiss, shoved her back slightly and dropped his head.

Her back arched and she released a little mew when his lips trapped one nipple and he sucked hard. Her fingers convulsed around his head with each pull of his mouth. He moved to the other one and did the same, but this time his teeth scraped the pebbled tip.

"Yes," she hissed. She rocked on his lap, needing him inside her. To fill that emptiness.

She released his head as he continued to suck, nip and tease her nipples. Dropping her hands, she wrapped her fingers around his hot length. Smooth like silk over steel, precum accumulated at the tip. Her thumb brushed over it and she began to stroke.

He sucked harder, his fingers finding her other ignored, aching nipple and giving it the attention it so needed until he gasped, her wet nipple slipping from between his lips. He shoved his face into her neck and groaned as she continued to stroke him, but now she also lightly cupped his balls, her fingers playing along the velvety soft skin.

"Baby," he groaned against her. Then his fingers were digging into the flesh of her hips and he was pulling her up and over him. She lined him up, the hot, swollen head of his cock pressing between her slick folds.

But she didn't sink down, even when he encouraged it. He grunted, lifting his hips ever so slightly, showing her what he wanted.

She wanted that, too.

But not until she was ready to give it to him.

She leaned forward and traced the outer shell of his ear with the tip of her tongue, then snagged his earlobe between her teeth and sucked it.

His breath was ragged, more precum beading, getting him ready.

"Baby," he moaned. "Jayde..."

"What do you want, Linc?" she whispered into his ear.

"You know what I want," he grumbled.

"Tell me," she urged softly.

"Rather show you." His voice was low and strained as he used his strength to pull her down, and when he did so, he filled her up. Completely.

Her eyes closed, her lips parted as the breath rushed out of her. She wrapped her arms around his shoulders and pressed her hard, aching nipples into his bare chest. She ground her hips in a slow circle to make sure he was fully seated.

He was.

"That's it, baby. Now ride me," he demanded in a rough voice, causing a shiver to skitter down her spine.

Her knees drilled into the leather of her backseat as she lifted and lowered herself on his length. "Like this?"

"Yeah. Fuck yeah, baby, just... like... that—" his voice broke.

His fingers kneaded her ass cheeks as she rose and fell, taking her time, keeping the pace slow, enjoying the way they fit together just right. Her head fell back and noises she couldn't help filled the tight interior of the car.

"You make me so fuckin' hard, Jayde..." He grunted.

She dropped her head forward, her hair falling around her face. He brushed it away and lifted her chin until they were eye to eye.

"That's what you fuckin' do to me. Been driving me nuts forever. Tried my fuckin' best to be smart. Stay away. But want you, Jayde, and you're hard to fuckin' resist."

"Stop resisting," she suggested, then pressed her lips along his shoulder, over his collarbone, up his neck. She nipped at his strong chin, then his bottom lip before taking his mouth once more. But only for a second. She pulled away enough to murmur, "Take what you want, Linc. I'm offering it to you. I'm giving myself to you."

"Ain't that easy, baby. It ain't and you know it."

She ignored that and pressed her cheek to his, tightening the hold she had on his shoulders. She began to move faster, to distract him, because she didn't want to hear what he had to say right now.

One of his hands slipped between them and he rolled her nipple between his fingers, making her gasp in his ear. He didn't stop and every time he twisted, it sent an electric pulse to her core. She clenched around him and he grunted as he thrust up hard, their flesh smacking loudly. He dropped his hands to grab both of her ass cheeks and, with a sudden desperation, he took over. His rhythm was fast, hard and relentless. He pounded her as hard as he could in that position and she accepted him all, even as deep as he was going.

"Linc," she cried out.

"That's it, baby. Cry out my name. Wanna feel how wet you get when you come. Wanna feel that heat explode 'round me. Want you to remember me making you come that hard and no one else."

No one else.

Those words, what seemed like a claim, was all it took to send her tumbling over the edge.

"Ah, fuck," he groaned as her whole body convulsed around him, her nails digging into his back.

She felt a rush of wetness and it wasn't from him. No... it was from her. His head fell back against the seat, his body stiffened and with one last lift of his hips, he came with a low grunt, his fingers squeezing her ass so hard they might leave marks.

A moment later, after the root of his cock stopped throbbing, he collapsed in the seat and Jayde fell against his chest, putting all her weight on him. They both fought for breath, her pulse pounding. Their bodies were damp with sweat and Jayde didn't want to move.

Apparently, neither did Linc. They sat that way for the longest time in the dark, and now quiet car. She didn't move until her muscles began to complain. She lifted her head from where she was listening to his heartbeat. "Thank you."

His head jerked. "For what?"

"For showing me I wasn't wrong."

His brows furrowed low. "'Bout what?"

"Us."

"Jayde," he growled, his body going solid beneath her. "Sex. Nothing more."

"No."

"Yes," he said more firmly.

She wasn't going to argue with him. He knew it was more. He just didn't want to admit it.

And she understood why. The cards were stacked against them. And this pregnancy wasn't going to make any of it easier. Not in the least.

His body relaxed again and hers melted against his as his breathing steadied. He said nothing for the longest time. Then he pressed his forehead to hers and released a long, slow breath as he swept a lock of her hair off her shoulder, his fingers trailing down her back. "Sorry, baby. Didn't mean to upset you earlier by saying I don't wanna kid with you. Just don't want you making the wrong choice. And being with me is the wrong fuckin' choice. Got a good life and a better one ahead of you. Don't want this to fuck all that up for you."

"Linc—"

"Once it's done and over, you'll agree it was the best decision."

Her stomach rolled and her chest felt like it collapsed. He still wanted her to terminate the pregnancy? After that?

Oh, that's right, it was just sex.

A burn bubbled up from the pit of her stomach. She straightened and pulled out of his arms, scrambling off him to shove the passenger door open and scream, "Get the fuck out of my car!"

He blinked. "What?"

She pointed outside the door. "I didn't fucking stutter. Get the fuck out of my car!"

"Jayde..."

"No. Get the fuck out. I'll do this shit on my own. Without you. Don't worry, I won't tell anyone who the father is. You're fucking safe."

"Jayde." He reached out to grab her arm, but she yanked it away.

Leaning naked over the passenger seat, she grabbed his clothes. Once she had them all gathered, she whipped them into his chest. "Get your shit and... GET. GONE!"

"Jayde!"

"No, Linc. Fuck you..."

CHAPTER THREE

"No, Linc. Fuck you... I'll take care of everything and not in the way *you* want me to. You won't owe me shit. You won't owe this baby shit. This will be *my* child, not yours, since you don't want it. Do you hear me? Mine. Now... Get. The. Fuck. Out. Of. My. Car!"

Jayde's words, full of hurt and anger, still rang in his ears. He stared down at the half-empty coffee mug in his hand, hoping it would give him some answers. It didn't.

He had gotten out of her car and put his clothes on as she drove away in a rage, still completely naked. She had squealed the tires as she drove out of the lot, leaving his ass in the dust. He'd walked the two long fucking miles back to The Iron Horse. He'd stupidly left his cell phone behind the bar when he dragged Jayde out of there three nights ago, so didn't have any way to call for a ride.

He hadn't heard from her since.

Now she was the one ignoring his texts and phone calls. She probably blocked his number. And he certainly wasn't going to her parents' house to knock on their fucking door.

The back door to church crashing open made Linc glance up. His grip tightened on his coffee mug as he took a step back before he could stop himself. But with his brain spinning, he braced.

Axel Jamison grabbed him by the throat, knocked his Harley mug to the ground making it shatter and hot coffee splash everywhere. Then his fist made direct contact with Linc's cheek.

Linc grunted at the impact as his head whipped back and his brain shook violently. His hands came up, one grabbing Axel's wrist and the other blocking the next blow, since Jayde's brother was holding him tight enough that Linc couldn't duck.

Even though they were about the same size, the fucker was stronger than he looked.

"What the fuck!" Linc yelled as he blocked one right hook, but couldn't block the next one.

With the direct impact to his sternum, he dropped to his knees, gasping for air, his hands going to his face and stomach as Jayde's cop brother released him.

Then a finger jabbed directly in his face. "You motherfucker!"

Linc glanced up at the man whose face was almost purple, his blue eyes narrowed, his jaw tight, and his nostrils flaring.

"You... You *motherfucker!*"

The man wasn't in uniform. He was wearing jeans and a tee. But that didn't mean Linc wouldn't be arrested for defending himself.

Linc grabbed a nearby bar stool and pulled himself to his feet, his eyes not leaving Axel, whose chest continued to heave.

Linc gathered the breath he lost with the uppercut. "I'll let you have those two. But you fuckin' hit me again and it's on," he growled as he wiped the back of his hand over his mouth. He studied the red blood that spread across his skin. The fucker had made him bleed.

"You shut the fuck up. I'm going to be the one doing the talking!" Axel roared in Linc's face.

"Got nothin' to say to you, pig," Linc roared back. When Axel took a step forward, Linc pushed his chest out and straightened his shoulders. He curled his fingers into loose fists and raised them slightly, ready to block and jab, if needed. "Ready for you now. Do your fuckin' best."

Out of the corner of his eye, Linc saw Crow running down the steps, as well as the back door open again and someone else rushing in.

Zak yelled across the room as he approached them. "What the fuck's goin' on?"

Axel jabbed a finger in Linc's direction, his eyes narrowed. "This motherfucker..."

Z stepped between them, facing Axel. "What about 'im?"

Axel's chest was still heaving as his gaze went from his older brother to Linc, who had enough sense now that his prez was there to stay quiet until he knew what the fuck was going on.

Unfortunately, he had a good idea what Axel's fury was about.

Axel shook a finger at Linc again. "This motherfucker..."

"What the fuck, Axel? Use your fuckin' words!" Z yelled, hands on his hips.

Axel stared at the floor, shook his head, then glared up at Z. "Jayde's pregnant."

Crow, who had moved behind Linc, made a low noise and Z's mouth dropped open. Then it snapped shut, his eyes now as hard as Axel's as they slid between his brother and Linc.

"What the fuck?" Zak muttered. "An' she said it was his?"

Axel shook his dark head again, blowing out a breath. "Fuck no. She wouldn't say whose it was. Just came to Bella and me, asking if we'd be interested in adopting the baby."

What?

"What?" Z echoed Linc's thought.

"Said she's just checking out her options. Hasn't told Mom or Dad yet. Said she won't until she figures out what she's doing first."

"What?" Z asked again, his gaze landing on Linc. "This true?"

Fuck.

He could be smart and play dumb, since Jayde never told Axel he was the father. Or he could man up. Which right now could be dumb, since he would have two pissed off brothers on his hands. He might get thumped within an inch of his life.

And he doubted Crow would take his back right now. The ink slinger wasn't stupid, either. Plus, he'd been a part of the club even longer than Z. Not to mention, he was super protective of the women. Linc was pretty sure that the man wasn't happy with Axel's news.

So, yeah, Crow wasn't going to help Linc's ass get out of this jam.

Z moved closer, leaning toward Linc. "You knock up my fuckin' sister?"

Ah, fuck. This was not going to be good. But lying would only make things worse.

"Says it's mine," Linc muttered.

Z jerked back and then spun away from him, shaking his head. He walked halfway through the common area, then spun back, his fingers raking through his shoulder-length hair. "That night. The night we couldn't find you two. Hawk's weddin'…"

Axel's gaze sliced to his older brother. "I knew shit was going down between them! I told you."

"An' I helped you fuckin' search, Ax, so calm your fuckin' tits," Z growled.

"How the hell can I *calm my tits*, when this asshole," Axel jabbed a finger in Linc's direction again, "one of *your* brothers, took advantage of Jayde."

"She…" Nope. Just fucking nope. Linc wasn't going to say it. Jayde had wanted it as much as him, if not more, but he was not going to throw her under the bus. He needed to drop his balls, be a man and take responsibility for this fuck-up. This *major,* life-changing fuck-up. "She say that?" Linc asked Axel's back, since the cop had turned away from him and was now staring a hole into who-knows-what he was glaring at.

"Doesn't fucking matter what she said. She's just a girl." Axel's growl that sounded just like his older brother's, along with his tight shoulders said it all.

Jayde could do no wrong.

"Jesus, Axel. She's fuckin' twenty-eight," Crow finally spoke up, stepping beside Linc. "Pissed as I am right now, gotta see reason. Jayde ain't a little girl anymore. She's responsible for her own actions."

Axel spun on his heels, that glare now pointed at Crow. "You have no say in this, Crow. It's family shit."

Crow's eyelids shuttered over his dark eyes and his jaw got tight. "Jayde's DAMC. She's family."

"She is *not* DAMC."

"It runs in her veins. Her granddad was a founder. Her brother is prez. An' now..." Crow glanced at Linc. "Now she's carrying one of the fourth generation."

"Holy fuck," Axel groaned, scrubbing a hand over his head. "Dad's going to have a coronary." His blue eyes landed on Linc. "He's going to kill you." He glanced at Z. "Dad's going to end up in prison for murder. Telling you now, Z. He's going to go ballistic."

"Yep," was all Z said, his brows furrowed as he stared at his boots, his arms crossed over his chest.

Yep?

"We fucked up," Linc finally admitted now that the coloring in Axel's face was more a normal shade.

"*We?*" Axel barked. "A real man would have made sure his woman was protected."

Fuck.

He opened his mouth to correct Axel and tell the cop that his sister wasn't his "woman." But that might make the man's face turn purple all over again. And Linc's sternum and cheek already hurt like fuck. The man seemed to be half-decent with his fists. Pig or not.

"I fucked up," he corrected.

"Jayde ain't his woman," Z said to Axel. "Or wasn't." He turned to Linc. "Is she? Have you two been goin' behind everyone's back?"

"No." Linc needed to handle this carefully. While he didn't want to throw Jayde under the bus, he also needed to explain shit to his prez. Fuck Axel. He didn't need to explain anything to that pig. But Z? Yeah. Z was his president and could get Linc's colors stripped off his back faster than he could say "positive pee stick."

"So you just used her?" Axel asked. His dark head spun toward Z. "Fuck Dad going to jail. *I'm* going to kill the fucker."

Z raised a palm. "Fuckin' calm the fuck down, Axel. Jesus Fuckin'

Christ. We've tolerated a lotta shit from you 'cause of Bella. You don't belong here in church. Weren't invited. So, you're an outsider an' only here due to my graciousness."

Oh fuck, that wasn't going to help Axel's temper.

The cop scowled at Z. "Jayde's my baby sister."

"Mine, too. An' Linc's my brother. So I'll deal with it."

Axel's head jerked back. "What? How the fuck are you going to deal with it?"

Z shrugged. "Dunno yet. Gotta talk to Jayde. Talk to Linc. Fuckin' figure this shit out."

Fuck.

"Did you not hear the part where I said she came to us and asked if we'd be interested in adopting the baby?"

"Fuck yeah," Z mumbled. "Heard it. Linc's got a say in this shit, too. His kid."

Axel's jaw dropped, then he snapped it shut. "Let me tell you something. Hearing that affected Bella. Hearing that someone didn't want their kid totaled her. I understand and appreciate what Jayde was trying to do, but it sent Bella into a tailspin that I," he slapped his palm against his own chest, "had to deal with."

"She okay?" Crow asked.

Axel's head twisted toward the ink slinger. "Now, yeah. Luckily."

"I offered..." Linc let that drift off. Now would not be a good time to let her brothers know just what he offered Jayde. Not if he wanted to keep breathing.

"What? What did you offer? To marry her? To move her into your room upstairs? To throw a baby seat onto the back of your bike? What? What do you possibly have to offer her?" Axel yelled, his arms flinging wide. He spun on Z. "She has two years left in law school, Z. *Law school.* Having a kid's going to fuck that all up. She's going to be tied to a fucking biker for the rest of her life through this kid. A kid she's in no way prepared to have."

"You don't give her enough credit," Crow muttered, then moved over to the commercial coffeemaker in the corner, grabbing his mug and filling it. He moved behind the bar and leaned against the back counter, taking a sip of his coffee as he contemplated the rest of them.

Linc needed to keep his eyes on Axel. The cop was the immediate threat, not Crow. That man didn't have a quick temper, but then Jayde wasn't his sister.

Axel snarled at Crow, "You think she's ready for what having this kid's going to bring down on her? You think it's easy with Bella and me? You think our father's just going to welcome that... that... one with open fucking arms? Welcome him into the family? Congratulate him with a fucking pat on the back?"

"Think you got a problem with it, too," Crow said softly.

Axel's spine snapped straight. "Yeah, I do. She could be successful. She's college educated, she has a decent job in Kiki's firm, even though Keeks is a defense attorney. And she was aspiring to follow in Keeks' footsteps. She was going to have a good career, a good future. Now what? She's going to be saddled with some loser's kid."

Linc's nostrils flared and his fingers curled into fists.

Axel wasn't done yet. "All because he couldn't keep his dick in his pants."

"Or a wrap on it," Crow muttered nearby.

Jesus fuck, Linc didn't need that kind of help from Crow.

"It's a mistake that'll get fixed," Linc said, shaking his head and moving to find a new mug and get more coffee. He definitely needed more caffeine. He'd have to get one of the sweet butts to clean up his shattered favorite mug, as well as the coffee off the floor later.

"That'll get *fixed?*" Axel echoed in a shout from behind Linc. "What the fuck does that mean?"

Linc sighed, since his answer wasn't going to make anyone in that room happy. As he reached for a clean mug, something hit him from the back and knocked him to the floor.

"Oh shit," Zak grumbled from somewhere other than the floor Linc found himself on.

The first blow struck Linc in the temple, scrambling his brain matter. He gathered his wits, or tried to, and twisted under Axel, but the cop straddled Linc as he was lying face-down on the concrete.

He planted his palms on the floor and with all his strength bowed his body up, tossing Axel off him. Linc was on his knees, then on his feet, as fast as Axel was.

"Fuck you, pig. Gotta take those fuckin' cheap shots." Linc raised his fists and spread his feet in a solid stance, even though his right ear was ringing. Linc blocked the next jab and delivered one of his own, striking Axel squarely in the nose. Blood spurted, but Axel ignored it. Linc dug deep, remembering everything Slade taught him when it came to boxing and self-defense.

Linc dodged Axel's next swing and landed a hook into the man's ribs. Axel doubled over with a pained grunt, but quickly recovered and rushed Linc with his head-down. Jayde's brother caught Linc in the chest, shoving him backwards straight into the table that held the coffeemaker.

Linc wrapped his hands around Axel's head and shoved him away just far enough to land an uppercut to his jaw. Axel's head flew up and back and he landed on his ass. Quickly scrambling to his knees, Axel fell forward, wrapping his arms around Linc's legs and taking him down to the ground once more.

Before he could roll out from underneath Axel, the man was gone and Z was hauling Linc up by his armpits. "You fuckers had enough, yet?"

Crow was holding Axel in a bear hug, and the cop was wincing at the tight hold. Good. Linc hoped he broke a couple ribs with that right hook.

"No!" Axel shouted, trying to pull from Crow's arms, blood trickling from his nose, over his mouth and down his chin. "I want to know what the fucker meant by *fixing* it."

"You ain't the only one," Z muttered.

Linc pushed at Z's arms, trying to get free. "Believe it or not, asshole, I want what's best for her, too. We— *Fuck!*" He scraped a hand over his hair. "I fucked up. *I fucked up.* I'll take the fuckin' blame. But I don't want her life fucked up, either. You're fuckin' right. She deserves a whole lot fuckin' better than me. Just like you said, a fuckin' loser. Don't got shit to offer her. Told her that. Told her she got a good life and not to let this fuck it up. She doesn't listen."

Z grunted behind him. "No shit."

The club prez finally released him and Linc braced himself as Crow let Axel go. But Axel just swiped a hand over his bloody lower face and stared at Linc. Axel sucked in a loud, long breath, then blew it out.

Crow moved back behind the bar, grabbed a wad of paper towels and offered it to Z's brother, who accepted it grudgingly.

"He's gonna be family, Axel. Can't be beatin' the shit outta each other," Crow said.

"Bullshit," Axel muttered, then he eyeballed Linc. "So you wanted her to have an abortion. That's what you're saying? Using the excuse that her life will be screwed up, even though terminating the pregnancy would save your ass?"

"Not saying I'm ready for a kid, 'cause I ain't. Not saying I don't wanna be with Jayde, either, but don't want to deal with your family. Wanna respect my prez—"

"Musta forgot that part when you stuck your dick in my sister," Z grumbled. "Didn't even ask me if you could see her on the regular. Definitely didn't ask if you could knock her the fuck up."

"Not seeing her on the regular—"

"Right, she's too good for you," Axel scoffed, shaking his head.

"Right. Don't wanna deal with," Linc waved his arm around, "this kinda shit. There's a lotta pussy where I ain't taking my life in my own hands. That's for fuckin' sure."

Axel's face got hard and Linc was pretty sure he fucked up again.

He quickly raised a hand. "Not saying she's just pussy. She ain't. Got a lot of things going for her. And that's why I suggested what I did. Just like you said, Axel, she doesn't need to be tied down to a loser."

"Ain't a loser," Z muttered, stepping between Linc and his real brother. He swung his head toward Axel. "He ain't a loser. Got a good head on 'im."

"Well, he certainly didn't use it if Jayde got pregnant."

"We all fuck up, Ax. *All* of us. You fucked up not believin' me 'bout bein' set up. Told you I was. Didn't believe it. Believed Dad's shit. Put a wedge between us. So, we *all* fuck up."

Axel dropped his head and shook it. When he finally raised it, he said, "Z, you got a raw deal. I know it now. I don't expect you to forgive me for that or to move past it. But we're talking about Jayde here. Our little sister. We're talking about her bringing a life into the world and her being responsible for it. She still lives with Mom and Dad, for fuck's sake."

"Probably not for long," Crow mumbled as he moved away to get another cup of coffee.

"Crow's right." Z's gaze landed on Linc. "Gotta step up. Do what's right. We all fuck up, but we all gotta fix our fuck ups. An' not the way you're thinkin'."

"Only want what's best for her," Linc stated one more time for those in the back who apparently weren't listening.

Axel shouted, "Should've thought about what was best for her before you stuck your dick in her! Jesus Christ!"

"But he did. An' it's done. Gotta move on from that," Crow muttered, then took another sip of coffee.

"Why the fuck are you still involved in this conversation?" Axel asked, both his eyes and arms wide.

Crow moved up to Linc and clapped a hand on his shoulder. "He's my brother. Jayde's a sister. Z's my brother, too. You forgot Linc was the one that threw himself over Jayde when the Warriors shot up The Iron Horse. Was willin' to take the hit instead of lettin' her. That's real fuckin' family, right there. You forgot what the hell real family was for over ten years, Axel. Fuckin' family sticks, got me?"

Axel threw up his hands, shook his head and then strode through the common room, shouting over his shoulder, "Figure it out, Z. Leaving it up to you to get this shit straightened out. And soon. Before Dad finds out."

Z gave him a two-finger salute that Axel never saw because he slammed out of the back door without a glance behind him. "Aye fuckin' aye, corporal."

Then Z turned his attention to Linc. Crow approached them, handed Linc a fresh mug of coffee, and said, "Gonna leave you two to figure shit out."

Linc watched as Crow went back upstairs and then he turned his full attention to his prez and began, "This club's everything to me, Z. Everything. Got nothing else. You guys got blood. Real blood. I just got all of you. Don't got shit to offer Jayde, this kid. Got my Harley and a fuckin' room upstairs. Can't haul a baby on a sled, can't raise a family in a ten by ten room."

Z didn't answer, instead he moved behind the bar, grabbed a shot glass and a bottle of Jack, pouring himself a double. He threw it back, hissed, then slammed the empty glass on the wooden bar top. "Gotta say, Linc, you're fucked."

That was one fact he already knew. "No shit," Linc muttered and approached the bar. "She's fuckin' pissed I suggested getting rid of the kid. Don't know what else to do."

"Be a man."

"Being a man by not wanting this to fuck up her life, brother. She's got goals. Dreams."

"An' you don't got shit," Z said before Linc could. "Keep sayin' that an' it's not true. You say you only got this club. But this club's fuckin' everything. It's all you need. We fuckin' got your back. But..." Z shook his head. "Fuckin' knockin' up the prez's sister ain't smart."

"Knocking up anyone's sister ain't smart," Linc agreed.

"Yeah, well..." Z sighed, poured himself another double and knocked that back, too. "Should be worried 'bout me. But I'm tellin' you now, Mitch is gonna be fit to be tied. Know it's hard for us to not think of her as a little girl any more. An' she ain't. Still... Mitch is never not thinkin' of her in that way. An' he already can't stand me. Can't stand this club. An' you just fucked 'im. Hard. Up the ass. Without lube." Z lifted a finger. "When he didn't want fucked."

Linc tried not to smirk at that description. Instead he dropped his head and stared at his coffee mug that he'd placed on the bar.

"Didn't mean to fuck up. Was trying to stay away from her. Trying to keep the peace with you and your folks. Didn't need the hassle."

"But?"

"But that night at Hawk's wedding... Not gonna get into details..."

"Right. Don't wanna hear 'em, either. You were here the day I got out of Fayette. You were here the night I fucked up with Sophie."

CHAPTER FOUR

L inc stared at the DAMC president. He remembered that day. The day Zak finally got released from prison. And the night of his "welcome home" party. He'd never met the man until then, since Linc had become a prospect only months prior to Z's release. But he'd heard about him. He'd heard a lot. How the man was progressive, how he'd wanted what was best for the club and his brothers. He'd also learned what had happened to him. What a fucked-up hand he'd been dealt. How his family deserted him, believing he was guilty since he was convicted.

Though he'd been set up, Axel and Mitch didn't believe it. Maybe they didn't even care. Everyone in the DAMC thought it had been the Shadow Warriors who set the prez up and the rival MC never claimed otherwise. That set-up got him arrested and sent to prison, effectively removing Z from the head of the table.

But it hadn't been the Warriors.

Fuck no. The traitor had been deeply embedded in the club. Had even been considered "family."

Those were two perfect examples of why you sometimes couldn't trust family. And finding out Pierce was the culprit rocked Linc to the core. Especially after thinking he finally found a home with his new "family." People who he could trust. *Brothers* for life.

Z kept talking, drawing Linc out of his thoughts. "An' I fucked up good. An', luckily, I fucked up *real good*. Best fuck up I ever did in my life. If I hadn't mistaken Sophie for a stripper an' dragged her ass upstairs..." Z shook his head and met Linc's gaze head-on. "I fucked up, brother. So fuckin' lucky I didn't end up back in that concrete palace for rape. Am one lucky motherfucker. An' can't say that enough. Love Soph to the ends of the earth. Hell, she gave me my son. Will give me future sons. Made my life whole, complete, after gettin' a raw fuckin' deal. She was the fuckin' light at the end of a long, dark tunnel. Got out an' knew my blood didn't give a rat's ass 'bout me but had the DAMC. Had my real brothers. An' you might not got a lotta shit besides your sled. Might not be rich scratch-wise. But you fuckin' got us. Yeah, you fucked up. An' you fucked up with your prez's sister, which could be a major offense. Could we strip your colors? Fuck yeah, we could. D an' Hawk don't know yet. They may freak the fuck out, they may not."

Linc snorted. D might just put him six feet under with one punch.

"But you ain't a loser. That's for fuckin' sure. Been nothin' but an asset to the club, to The Iron Horse. Fuckin' loyal. Hard worker. Like Crow said, you protected my sister when shit went down at the Christmas party. You woulda taken the bullets instead of her. That shit all means somethin' to me. To all of us."

"So, you ain't mad?" Linc asked carefully.

"Oh, I'm fuckin' pissed. Nothin' I can do 'bout it now." Z narrowed his eyes on Linc. "She ain't gettin' rid of it. Got what you were sayin', how it's gonna fuck up her life." He tapped his temple. "Got it. An' it's gonna cause a lotta fuckin' grief when it comes to Mitch. Think Axel was bad?" Z shook his head and blew out a breath. "*Fuck.* Mitch... He don't forgive or forget. Not even for his own fuckin' son."

Even after it came out that Pierce had set up Z, that Z never committed that crime, it hadn't fixed the relationship between Z and his cop father. Mostly because Mitch didn't know it was Pierce. Especially since the man mysteriously disappeared. No one wanted to try to explain that to a sergeant of the Shadow Valley Police Department. One who already had a hard-on for anything DAMC.

No matter what, Mitch still had issues with Z being part of the club. And he really had issues with Z sitting at the head of the table.

The man also had a serious problem with Baby Z being raised in the MC.

This whole situation could fuck Jayde up, not only with her career plans but with her father, for sure. Because if they did this, had this kid, there was no fucking way his kid was not being raised as an Angel. "What I gotta do to make this shit better?"

Z lifted a shoulder and let it drop. "Gotta talk to Jayde."

Linc had no idea if that meant he needed to talk to Jayde or Z did. "Won't talk to me. Think she's got me blocked."

"Blame her when you wanted her to get a fuckin' abortion?"

Linc rolled his eyes up to the ceiling for a moment. "No. Fucked up. Again." That suggestion had been a knee-jerk reaction to shocking news. But that news had simmered in his noggin for the past couple days, seeped into his bones. And he was looking at things a bit more clearly now. Sort of, anyway. No matter how he looked at it, though, the whole situation wasn't ideal.

Z whacked him on the back. "Yep. Probably gonna fuck up again, too. Loads more times. Dealin' with a woman. They're always thinkin' we've fucked up." Z's lips curled slightly at the ends. He poured another double and downed it with a wince before slapping the shot glass back on the bar. "We'll figure this shit out."

Linc stared at Z. "How?"

Z wiped the back of his hand over his mouth, then down over the short whiskers that covered his chin. "Club's got healthy coffers. Part of that's because you're good at managing The Iron Horse. Good at takin' direction from Hawk. No matter what, you're DAMC. Jayde is, too, whether Mitch wants to see it or not. If she's Bear's granddaughter an' the prez's sister, then she's DAMC. Club can set you up in a place. You an' her. Float you 'til you figure shit out. But gotta want it. Gotta be serious 'bout my sister. About this kid. Are you?"

Linc wasn't sure about all that. He wasn't ready to settle the hell down. Ol' lady. A kid. A place more than the room above church. Life was easy right now. He woke up, rolled out of bed, headed downstairs for grub, booze, pussy, whatever. Hit the bar at night for work.

Shit was easy.

Shit was going to change.

He wasn't sure if he was ready for that. For actual responsibility. Other than managing The Iron Horse and making sure his sled was kept in top-notch running condition. He wasn't ready to take on the responsibility of a fucking *family*.

And he wasn't going to let Jayde's being pregnant fuck up her chance at becoming an attorney. No fucking way. He wasn't going to be the reason she ended up disappointed on where she landed in life.

He couldn't do that to her. She didn't deserve that.

Even though they originally spotted each other years ago, while in their early twenties—her not long out of college, him a wet-behind-the-ears prospect—both had matured since then. He watched Jayde while it happened. And he felt it in his own bones, too.

But still... Have they both grown enough to be responsible for another life? And was he ready to take Jayde on as his ol' lady? Did he even want to?

And *fuck*... Was he going to be stuck in the middle of a shotgun wedding when those two shotguns were held by cops?

The blood rushed from his face and his head began to swim. Worse than when Axel punched him in the temple.

For fuck's sake, he might be tied to Jayde for the rest of his fucking life! Tied to one fucking woman.

His heart thumped in his chest and his legs turned to jelly, forcing him to grab a nearby bar stool to lean against it.

"Had to fight for my ol' lady. Convince her that she needed me. You ready to fight for Jayde?"

Holy fuck, was he?

No, he wasn't. He wasn't. Fuck no. *Fuck.* "Yeah," got caught in his throat and he had to clear it. "Yeah." Because what the hell else did you tell her brother who was his *fucking president?*

Z smiled. "Like I said, gonna figure this shit all out. No reason this kid should fuck up Jayde's chances on becomin' a lawyer. Plus, an extra club lawyer couldn't hurt, that's for fuckin' sure. We keep Kiki way too fuckin' busy, even in areas that ain't her expertise."

That was certainly true. Hawk's woman ended up working on legal issues other than criminal defense. Shit she didn't specialize in, but was needed. Whether it was for family law or business law. Whatever the club needed, she handled it. She really needed Jayde's help.

Even though Linc thought Diesel might pound him six feet under, it could very well be Hawk. The VP wanted to relieve some of Kiki's burden. Especially now that she just had Ashton, and who knew if they would have more kids down the road.

"So, when Mitch fuckin' disowns her, the club will make sure her education's paid for. Then she'll work for the club. It'll be an investment. No need for you to take on that financial burden."

Oh, thank fuck.

"Gotta get you set up somewhere big enough for three. Me, Soph an' Baby Z are startin' to outgrow the apartment above the bakery. Now with Vi here, D an' Jewelee are outgrowin' the apartment over the pawn shop. Fuck, we should set up some sorta housin' complex. Like that cul-de-sac of houses on Sister Wives." A snort burst from him. "Fuckin' Soph's glued to the fuckin' TV when that shit comes on. Told her if she wants a sister wife, I'm fine with it."

Jesus, Linc didn't want one fucking wife, forget two. Or more. "Ace said that's what the cabins on the farm were originally for."

"Yeah, that's fuckin' true. Annie got one, Allie got another. Diamond an' Slade got another. D's thinkin' of movin' into one a tenant just moved outta. But the rest are rented. Kinda far outta

town, too. Real convenient livin' over the bakery, 'specially with
Zeke. Sucks to hafta move."

"Would be safer to have everyone close by, 'specially on
Ace's farm."

"Yeah," Z breathed. "True."

"'Specially when it comes to the kids."

"That's true, too." Z tilted his head. "Gonna hafta think on that.
Build some sort of compound, maybe. Bella an' Axel need to stop
rentin', too. Maybe it's time for the DAMC to get into real estate."
He rubbed his forehead and sighed. "Whatever. Will talk about that
shit at the next executive meetin'. For now, just find a fuckin' place.
You don't got the scratch, then lemme know. Club will rent it. Need
to do it before Mitch finds out, otherwise Jayde may find herself
livin' in that fuckin' Camaro of hers. *If* he doesn't take her cage
back, too."

Jesus. Linc never even considered that Mitch would go as far as
taking back her car from her and leaving her without a ride.

Z continued, "He does that, Crash will hafta get her somethin' to
hold 'er over."

Thank fuck for this club.

"What about her not takin' my calls and shit? Hard to talk to her,
work shit out when she ain't talkin' to me."

Z stared at him for a long minute, then pulled a cell phone out of
his back pocket, stabbed at it a few times with his finger before
putting it up to his ear. "Jayde. Yeah. No. Axel's pissed. Yep. Fuck.
Yep. Yep. Fuck. No. Fuck! Shut the fuck up for a second, will ya?
Jesus." Z sighed and rolled his eyes. "Yeah. Nope. Just Crow.
Listen..." He sighed again, pulled the phone away from his head and
made a face at it before putting it back to his ear. "Gonna listen?
Jayde, listen. Fuckin' listen. Jesus fuckin' Christ!" He blew out a
breath. "Be at my apartment at eight, got me? After the bakery
closes. Fuckin' Jayde, just fuckin' be there. Don't give me lip, woman.
Eight! Bakery!" He jabbed at his phone multiple times, his jaw tight
and mumbling a curse, then shoved it back in his pocket. "Fuckin'

women! Motherfuckin' Christ!" Z took a good look at Linc, then smirked. "Good fuckin' luck with that one."

Right.

"Be at my apartment. Eight. Got me?"

Right.

Linc's fingers clawed at his throat. The invisible noose around his neck suddenly became extremely tight.

CHAPTER FIVE

J ayde swiped a cupcake off the tray on the counter. Raising it, her eyes landed on Sophie who was sitting on the floor playing with Zeke. Toys were strewn all over the carpet, turning their small living room into an obstacle course.

"Double chocolate with a mousse center," Sophie answered Jayde's unspoken question, while handing Baby Z another small dump truck, since he had quickly gotten bored with the thousands of trucks, cars and other toys he was previously playing with.

Jayde peeled the paper off the bottom of the cupcake and shoved half of it into her mouth. Her stomach felt like a bottomless pit lately.

Her older brother was standing at the windows along the back of the apartment that looked down onto the stone parking lot at the rear of the bakery. The hairs on the back of her neck prickled. "Who are you waiting for, Z?"

She knew. She fucking knew. *Son of a bitch*.

"What did you do?" she whispered fiercely, setting the half-eaten cupcake onto the counter and moving up to Zak. She shoved his shoulder. "What did you do? I thought this was going to be a family meeting!"

Z turned toward her and the same blue eyes she saw every day in the mirror met hers. "Gonna be a family meetin'," he muttered.

"Then you're waiting for Axel, right?" she asked, hopeful. She turned from the windows to look at Bella, who sat on the couch, arms crossed over her chest, her long dark hair still up in a neat bun from working downstairs in the bakery all day. "Ax is coming, right?" she asked her brother's fiancée.

"Yeah, he's coming. But he's working, so I'm not sure when he can stop in," Bella finally said.

Jayde's eyes widened, and she shoved Z again, panic crawling up her throat. "You didn't invite Mom and Dad!"

Z's lips flattened out. "Fuck no."

"Then there's no reason for you to be standing there unless you invited Linc."

"Right," Z muttered.

"Zak, no! Why?" Jayde cried, and spun away from the windows. "Why would you do that?"

Z's face got dark and his blue eyes narrowed as he turned to face her, his hands planted on his hips. "Because it's his fuckin' kid, that's why. Go sit the fuck down."

"He wants nothing to do with it. He wanted me to..." She hissed out a breath. She didn't want to have that conversation all over again in front of Bella. After Jayde had left their house that night, Axel had to deal with Bella having a mental meltdown. And she didn't want to cause Bella to have another one. Especially without Axel nearby.

She loved Bella. They were like sisters. Jayde had thought the option of allowing Axel and Bella to adopt her baby was a good one. The baby would stay in the family and Jayde would get to be at least an "aunt," be involved with her child. Bella could never have kids of her own and Jayde knew that she and Ax wanted one. If they were going to end up adopting anyway, why not one that was blood?

The baby would have two loving parents that way, right?

Maybe it was the shock of finding out Jayde was pregnant in the first place that had caused Bella to spin out of control. Jayde should have prepared Axel first, but she also knew he'd be pissed. So she had decided to rip off the Band-Aid all at once.

And, once again, she made the wrong decision and fucked up.

She sighed. "I'm not sure what good this is going to do."

"Gonna come up with a fuckin' plan, that's what we're gonna do. Linc's gonna hafta step up—"

"What!" Jayde screamed, which made Zeke yell in excitement, then laugh. She glared down at her nephew. "This isn't funny, kid. This is serious!"

In answer, Zeke raised a chubby fist at her and smiled.

"Jayde, calm down," Bella murmured. "We know what Linc wanted and we understand why. He's just looking out for you."

Jayde turned wide eyes to her. "Are you shitting me? He's looking out for me? He's looking out for himself."

Sophie mumbled, "I have to agree with Jayde on that point."

"Having a baby is going to change your life. Change your path," Bella said calmly.

Jayde swung a hand toward Z. "Sophie and Zak's doing just fine with it."

Bella sighed impatiently. "The bakery was already established, Jayde. With me and Z helping, and now the baker's helpers, it's not a hardship for them to have kids at this point."

"Having help definitely makes it easier," Sophie agreed. She got to her feet and started to gather the scattered toys and put them into a painted, wooden box. Zeke pushed himself off the floor, toddled over to the open box and every toy Sophie put away, he pulled back out and threw it on the floor with a grunt.

Like father, like son.

With a snort, Z grabbed Baby Z. "C'mon, bud, you piss your momma off an' your old man might not be gettin' any later."

"Zak!" Sophie scolded him, shaking her head as she continued to clean up the floor.

Zeke laughed, slapped Z on his bearded cheek and said, "Dada. Truck!"

"Nope, bud, momma's gotta clean up. Uncle Ax is comin'."

"Ax!" Zeke screamed and his whole body jerked in Z's arms with excitement.

"At least you aren't calling him Uncle Pig," Bella said.

"He'll learn that soon enough," Zak answered.

It was hard to miss the roar of the straight pipes approaching the back of the bakery. Instantly Jayde's heart began to thunder almost as loud as Linc's exhaust.

"Vroom vroom," Baby Z crowed.

Zak carried him back to the window and pointed outside. "Yep. Vroom vroom just like Dada's sled."

"Mota sickle, Dada."

"Yep, mota sickle, bud. You an' me on my mota sickle. Soon."

Sophie made a noise and slammed the lid shut on Zeke's toy box. "No. Not soon."

Z's eyes slid to his wife. "Soon."

Sophie made a face and settled into a nearby recliner with a huff.

As Jayde heard the sled shut down, she rushed back over to the counter and shoved the remaining half of the cupcake into her mouth. There weren't enough cupcakes in the world right now to settle her churning stomach, or lower her rising blood pressure.

"Gonna go get Linc. Need to stay here bud." He put Baby Z on the floor and the eighteen-month old stomped around, rushing in Bella's direction. Bella held out her hands and Zeke face planted into her lap with a chortle.

"That's my boy, learnin' young."

"Zak!" Sophie yelled.

Jayde's brother only laughed, shook his dark head and headed out the door.

Jayde wanted to escape, but the apartment only had one way in and out. And if she left now, Zak would stop her. She had no idea what any of this would solve.

"Did you know he invited Linc?" she asked Bella and Sophie.

"You blocked his calls, his texts," Sophie simply said.

"There was a reason for that!" Jayde proclaimed.

"Well, how can you guys figure things out if you're not communicating?"

Jayde stared at Sophie. "If he doesn't want the baby, he doesn't get to make decisions."

"Jayde," Bella said softly. "Linc is family. Even if your brother and I decide to step in and adopt your baby, Linc would have to agree to that."

Jayde's head spun toward Bella. "You two are considering that?"

"We've discussed it. But until you two sit down and talk like adults, make rational decisions, we're not discussing it any further."

"So you want us to talk about it in front of all of you?" Jayde cried out, the panic sweeping through her all over again. They expected Linc and her to have a discussion with an audience? Not just an audience, but a very opinionated one who would probably keep interjecting.

"Maybe if we all put our heads together, we can come up with a good solution for everybody," Sophie suggested.

Put their heads together? "For fuck's sake, it's a baby, not a NASA mission," Jayde hissed.

"Sometimes dealing with a baby is like dealing with a launch. Especially when it comes to diapers and... I'll just mention the words projectile and fluids. I'll leave the rest to your imagination. You'll know soon enough." Sophie snickered.

Bella made a noise and Jayde's attention was drawn to the couch. Zeke was determined to crawl into Bella's lap, but she held onto his hands, making him stand on the floor between her legs. While she was getting better with the baby, it was taking time.

Jayde knew Bella wanted to be better, wanted to cuddle Zeke and Violet, and even Ashton. Everyone could see it in her eyes. But it remained a struggle for her.

Understandably so.

To have someone murder your unborn child...

Hell, to have the person you were supposed to trust and love—the father of that baby—murder his own child, and try to murder his own wife...

Axel had mentioned Bella was now in therapy for her PTSD. Hopefully that would help. Especially if they wanted to adopt a baby in the near future.

Bella's face got tight as Zeke tried to climb up her legs. Before Sophie could rise from the recliner to stop him, Jayde rushed over and snagged him, picking him up.

"Whatcha doin', Z-bear?" she cooed to her nephew.

"Jay-jay," he squealed as she spun in a circle with him in her arms. She began to laugh as loudly as he was.

Linc stopped in the doorway as Z pushed through, heading into the apartment. His gaze froze on Jayde, who was swinging Zeke around in her arms, a smile on her face as she looked down at the baby, while Baby Z was shrieking with unadulterated glee.

Jesus fuck.

His heart had to have stopped because suddenly it went into overdrive, thumping like a bass drum in his chest. This could be her with his kid. Swinging his kid around while laughing and appearing happy. He grabbed the door frame as the blood rushed into his ears like a freight train.

Z stopped and glanced over his shoulder. "What the fuck you waitin' for? Close an' lock the door."

Jayde spun to a stop at her brother's words and, when her blue eyes landed on Linc, she quickly lost her smile.

Fuck. He did that. He stole that beautiful, natural smile from her.

He shook himself loose and stepped into the apartment, shutting and locking the door behind him.

With a frown, Jayde carried Zeke over to his father and handed him off. Then she plopped down on the couch next to Bella, crossing her arms over her chest.

That was not a good sign that she'd be willing to discuss this whole fucking thing.

Zak, shifting Zeke in his arms, grabbed a couple bottles of Iron

City beer from the fridge and handed one to Linc. "Probably gonna need that."

"Yeah," Linc grunted, twisting off the cap and lifting the bottle to his lips, letting the cold brew slide down his throat. He wiped his mouth with the back of his hand before moving deeper into the room.

Z plunked his son into Sophie's lap, then pulled two stools from the kitchenette into the living area and flipped a hand toward one. "Sit."

Linc sat. But as soon as he did, his knee began to bounce up and down. Jayde glaring at him from across the room didn't help.

He chugged down another mouthful of beer, then cleared his throat. "Jayde—"

A pounding on the door had all eyes turning in that direction.

"It's me," came muffled through the door.

Zak got up and let Axel in. The man was in uniform, so maybe they wouldn't get into a knock-down battle tonight. Linc still sported bruises from the last one. The worst one had bloomed under his right eye. Slade had given him shit for taking punches from Axel and not blocking every single one of them. He said his training had gone to waste. It hadn't, but Linc wasn't going to argue with the man.

Linc had his beer bottle hanging from two fingers between his thighs as he cautiously watched the cop adjust his duty belt with a yank and then settle on the couch on the other side of Bella. He curled fingers around his ol' lady's jaw, pulled her to him and pressed a kiss to her forehead.

"Hey, baby," he greeted her.

"Quiet shift?" she asked softly, a small smile curling her lips.

"Yeah. Everything good here?"

"So far," she answered. "Linc just got here and hasn't said a damn word yet, so that might change."

Everyone's eyes turned to Linc and he straightened on his stool. He scraped fingers through his hair.

Fuck. Was he supposed to start? "I—"

"Gotta figure this shit out before Mitch does," Zak spoke up.

"Agreed," Axel said. He leaned forward and looked at his sister at the other end of the couch. "Because life's going to blow up for you once he finds out. Better get all your fucking ducks in a row first."

"Yeah, it'll suck sleepin' in the back seat of that Camaro," Z added with a smirk.

Linc was so glad his president found this shit amusing.

"I'll get my own place," Jayde said, her chin held high.

"Sure fuckin' are," Z said, his amusement gone.

"What are you talking about?" she asked him, her eyebrows furrowed low.

"Told you we're figurin' this shit out."

"I'm twenty-eight years old. Do you think I need my brothers figuring things out for me?"

"Yes!" came from both Z and Axel in unison.

Jayde's lips pressed together and she frowned. "Whatever." She flipped a hand toward Linc. "We already know what he wants... or *doesn't* want, more like it."

"Jayde," Sophie murmured. "Please. This is important."

Jayde closed her eyes and something crossed her face before she dropped her head and nodded. "I know," she whispered. She lifted her head, her eyes shiny as they stared at Linc. "This is very important." She chewed on her bottom lip.

Jesus, she was going to wreck him. He wanted to cross the room, rip her off that couch and into his arms. Tell her everything was going to be fucking all right. Hold her tight, kiss her forehead like Axel did to Bella and assure her that he'd be there for her through this whole fucking thing. He'd be by her side and—

His jaw tightened as Axel broke into his thoughts. "Let's go through this step-by-step, shall we?" He glanced around the room and when no one answered, he continued, "First, carry the baby to term or not?"

"Of course!" Jayde exclaimed.

Everybody's eyes slid to him. They were waiting for his answer. Linc sat there silent for a second as he closed his eyes and pictured Jayde holding Zeke earlier. "Whatever Jayde wants."

Linc didn't miss the knee squeeze Axel gave Bella. With a sharp nod of approval, Jayde's brother continued. "Give the baby up for adoption or keep the baby?" Before Jayde could answer, he said, "If you two decide to give the baby up, then Bella and I are taking him or her. No exceptions." Bella covered Axel's hand on her knee and this time she squeezed. She wasn't looking at anyone, only stared at the floor.

Linc's gaze slid to Jayde and he realized she was eyeballing him. Hard. With narrowed eyes.

Fuck.

He tried to swallow the lump in his throat, but it was determined to stick right where it had landed.

Suddenly, all the trepidation he'd been feeling about this meeting, all the dread that had twisted his gut for days, sluiced off him like a cold shower. He shook himself mentally to rid himself of any remaining doubt.

Fuck. This. Shit.

He placed his beer bottle on the floor next to the stool and jumped to his feet. With three long strides, he was at the couch, grabbing Jayde's arm and pulling her from it.

"What—" she squeaked in surprise.

Axel jumped up from the couch, his hand landing on his holster.

Z's stool fell backwards with a clatter as he stood quickly. "What the fuck!"

Linc lifted a palm. "Just need to talk to Jayde. *Alone.*" Then he began to drag her across the room and toward the door.

"No. I've got nothing to say to—"

"We're talking and doing it right fuckin' now. And not in front of your fuckin' family. No one else's making decisions for us. No one knows what's fuckin' best for us but us. Got me?"

Her mouth dropped open and he didn't wait for her to respond. He yanked open the door and pulled her through it.

"You can talk down in the bakery!" Sophie yelled. "We'll make sure the boys stay up here and leave you two alone."

With a grunt, Linc slammed the door shut and pointed down the steps. "Go. Now."

"But—"

"No lip, woman. Fuckin' go downstairs. Go!"

With a frown and pursed lips, she made her way carefully down the stairs, through the bakery's kitchen and out into the dark shop. He followed closely behind, picking up whiffs of her scent as she moved. Something sweet and light.

She started to reach for something on the wall, but he stopped her. He grabbed her wrist and spun her around, slamming her into his chest. He moved her back until she was pinned against the wall and then he dropped his head until his lips were right above hers.

"You listen to me, woman, and you listen good. If you fuckin' think you're having my kid and then giving it up... Fuck that. No fuckin' way, Jayde. No one else's raising my kid but me. You got me?"

Her warm breath came out in little puffs, sweeping over his lips. Her chest rose and fell quickly and even in the dark he could see the whites of her eyes.

"Nobody's raising our kid but you and me. You fuckin' *got me?*" He pointed toward the ceiling. "'Specially not that pig upstairs. You. Fuckin'. Got. Me?"

"Y-yes," she whispered. "But you said—"

"Know what I fuckin' said. Fucked up. Gonna fuck up plenty more fuckin' times, Jayde. Just expect it now so you're prepared and ain't disappointed. I'm gonna fuck up. Guaranteed. Doesn't mean I don't fuckin' want you. Doesn't mean I don't want our kid. *Fuck,*" he barked in frustration.

"But—"

"Yeah, baby," he breathed. "Just said I fucked up, so shut up and kiss me."

He didn't wait for her to comply, but took her mouth instead, crushing his lips to hers, finding her tongue with his, capturing her groan. His whole body relaxed when she melted against him, her hands crawling up his back under his cut, her nails digging into his flesh through his worn T-shirt.

Fuck, he wanted to feel those nails raking across his bare skin. But here and now was not the time or the place.

Z was right, he needed his own place. And he needed it yesterday.

They were going to have a kid and they needed to do it right. He wanted his kid raised properly and not fucked in the head because of his parents being stupid fucks. Being stubborn. Fighting over stupid shit.

Fuck no. If they were doing this, they were definitely doing it right. He knew everyone in the club would be supportive, have their backs, help them out, if needed. But he really wanted to do this on his own. Show Jayde he *could* do this.

Prove to her that he was worthy of her. To never regret their mistake.

Because, yeah, her getting pregnant was a big fucking mistake.

But he was going to make it right.

He was.

And he was going to make sure her life wasn't fucked because of it. He'd do whatever he needed to do to make sure her fucking dream of becoming a lawyer happened. This kid wasn't going to hold her back. If he needed to lean on Z, his brothers, the club to do it, then he was going to swallow his fucking pride and just do it. For Jayde.

For their kid.

Fuck!

He slammed a palm against the wall when his knees began to buckle. He sucked a sharp breath through his nose, then pressed his forehead to hers. "Gonna get a place. Gonna do this right, Jayde. Swear we're gonna do it right. *Gotta* do it right."

Her hands cupped his cheeks and she kept his forehead pinned to hers. "Are you sure?" Her voice sounded thick, like she was crying.

"Yeah. Never been so sure 'bout anything in my life, baby. Never. I knew this club was for me. And the fuckin' moment I saw you swinging those hips across that room, knew you were fuckin' mine.

Did my damnedest not to do you wrong. Fucked that up, but gonna make it right."

"So you keep saying."

"Promising you..."

"Okay," she said softly. "But..."

He lifted his head. "But what?"

"How are we going to tell my dad?"

Fuck.

CHAPTER SIX

Linc rolled over with a groan, his hand automatically going under the sheet to scratch his balls. Then he heard whatever it was that woke him the fuck up again. The muffled ring of his cell phone was coming from the floor.

He rolled some more and found his jeans next to the bed where he shucked them just a few hours ago after crawling in between his sheets, exhausted from working a long, busy night at The Iron Horse.

"Fuck," he muttered when he saw that it was Jayde blowing up his phone. He'd somehow slept through three phone calls from her. He slid his finger across the screen, and sitting up, he pressed it to his ear.

"Hey," he croaked, his voice rough with sleep.

"Linc..." She sounded like she was crying.

Linc's spine snapped straight and every nerve in his body went on high alert. "What's wrong?"

"Linc..." she said again and, fuck, followed it up with a big sob.

He pushed the tangled sheet off his lap and climbed out of bed. "What? What's going on?"

"They can't find it."

What the fuck was she talking about? "Find what?"

"The baby's heartbeat."

"What?" he yelled into the phone, his heart pounding. "Where the fuck are you?"

Her voice shook as she said, "At the doctor's. I had my first appointment."

"Why the fuck didn't you tell me? I woulda taken you!"

She sniffled into the phone. "I didn't think you'd want to come."

What the fuck?

"And there's no baby?"

"I don't know. They couldn't find the heartbeat. They said I'm definitely pregnant, but... but..."

Linc scrubbed a hand over his hair and dropped his head to stare at his bare feet. He didn't know what to say. "Jayde... I..."

"They want me to go over to another imagining center because they can't squeeze me in here today."

His brows furrowed in confusion. "For what?"

"An ultrasound."

"Where?"

"In Baldwin."

"Jesus. That far?"

"Yeah, I... I need you to come with me. I'd ask my mom, but..."

Right, they still didn't know. They were waiting to drop that bomb once they had a place lined up.

Linc blew out a breath. "Yeah, yeah. Of course. I'm gonna take you. I shoulda been there, Jayde. Shoulda told me."

"I know. I'm sorry. I know you don't want—"

"Jayde!" he yelled into the phone, cutting off whatever she was going to say next. Because he didn't want to hear it. "Gonna come get you."

"No. They can't get me in for another two hours. I'll go home first. I need to drink a bunch of water."

"Ain't picking you up at your pop's place," he growled. *Jesus.* He'd probably be shot on sight.

She was silent for a moment.

"Jayde, meet me downstairs at church. Gotta shower. Gotta wake up. Need to get some coffee in me. Then we'll go. Yeah?"

"Yeah," she whispered into the phone. "Linc..."

"No, don't even think like that. Everything's gonna be okay. Got me?"

"Linc..."

He softened his voice and tried to remain calm. "Everything's gonna be okay, baby. I promise."

Again, silence on the other end of the phone.

His stomach churned. "Baby, listen to me, I promise. Just get here as soon as you can."

He pulled the phone away from his ear to see she had disconnected. He whipped the phone onto the bed as hard as he could and screamed, "Fuck!" to the ceiling.

He just made another fucking mistake by promising her something he didn't have any control over.

The ultrasound technician entered the room, flipped off the lights and moved toward the bed where Jayde had her pants pulled down slightly and a sheet tucked into her waistband. She had her shirt pulled up and her tummy exposed.

She was trying not to cry. She didn't want to start because if she did, it was going to get ugly with a whole bunch of blubbering and snot bubbles. Linc was squeezing her hand so tightly that she was trying to use his strength to keep herself together.

Linc promised that everything was going to be okay, so she had to believe that it would be.

And besides his hand, that's all she had to hang on to.

"So, the doctor said he had a bit of a difficult time finding your baby's heartbeat."

Jayde couldn't even answer the tech, because her jaws felt as if they were fused together.

The woman turned on the machine next to the bed and began to squirt some warm gel onto Jayde's belly. "Let me take a quick look-see and then I'll turn on the TV up on the wall, so you can see what I'm seeing. Sound good?"

Linc jerked her hand in response. "No. Turn it on now. Need to see."

The tech froze, and her wide-eyed gaze landed on Linc. "But—"

"Turn it on," he growled.

Jayde squeezed his fingers. "Please. Let him watch. We're worried."

The tech stared at Jayde for a moment, then nodded. "Fine." She went over, switched on the large screen and came back to the ultra-sound machine and picked up the wand. "Okay, let me take a peek."

Jayde closed her eyes as the tech rolled the wand over her stomach, pressing, circling for what seemed like forever without saying a word. Every time the woman moved it around it didn't help her full bladder, which felt as though it was about to burst.

"Okay, yes, I see something. Right there. See that, Dad?"

Jayde heard no response from Linc. She opened her eyes and turned her head toward the screen. The one that Linc was staring at intently, his nostrils flaring.

"That's our baby," Jayde whispered, tears making her sight blurry as they welled up.

"Sure is. From what I can see, the baby is viable. It's too early to tell what sex the baby is, but let's find the heartbeat."

A few moments later, a wishy-washy sound, along with a strong steady heartbeat filled the room. Relief swept through Jayde as she continued to stare at the screen of the child she and Linc made together. She listened in awe to the thump, thump, thump of their baby's heart beating strongly.

"I'd say you're only about eleven weeks, right? Sometimes the heartbeat is hard to pick up on the Doppler in a doctor's office at that stage. But everything sounds and looks fine to me at this point. Only twenty-nine weeks to go!" She laughed lightly. "I promise it'll go fast. And next thing you know, you'll have a newborn in your arms."

Jayde blinked at that last part. She tried to picture herself with an infant. With the child she was seeing on that big screen in her arms.

Suddenly, everything seemed so real. This was really happening. They were actually having a child in twenty-nine weeks!

"I'm scared," Jayde whispered.

"Me, too," Linc answered back, still staring at the screen. She hadn't even realized she said that out loud until he answered.

"I'm sure you two will be fine." The tech had shut off the machine, patted her shoulder and then held out something to her.

"What's that?" she asked the tech.

"The images for you to keep."

Linc's head swung around at her words, since the TV had gone black and he stared at what Jayde clutched in her hand. "It's what?"

"Pictures," Jayde answered, lifting them. He released her hand and snagged them from her fingers.

"Of what?"

Jayde's lips twitched. "The baby."

His brows furrowed as he stared at the printed-out images in his hands. "Pictures of my son?"

"Or daughter," the tech said as she finished putting things away. "You can sit up and get dressed. I cleaned you off as best as I could with the towel, but here are some wipes if you need them." She tilted her head toward another door. "Restroom's there, because I'm sure that you need that, too."

She certainly did. She had drunk a ton of water. And the vibrations of Linc's sled didn't help with her full bladder on the trip over.

"You can find your way out?" The tech asked as she stared at Linc, still mesmerized by the sonogram images in his hands.

"Yes," Jayde said to her with a smile. She swiped at her cheek to remove the stray tear that had escaped. "Thank you for squeezing us in."

"You're very welcome." The tech patted her knee. "I'm happy for you two." On her way out of the room, she turned the lights back on.

"Are you okay?" Jayde asked Linc when he didn't say anything for the longest time.

He slowly lifted his gaze to meet hers. "Yeah," he said so softly that she almost couldn't hear it.

"I was so worried."

"Yeah."

"Everything's good now."

"Yeah, baby. Everything's just fuckin' great." And with that he crushed his lips to hers.

They were on a "date." An actual date. Or at least, that's what Linc was calling it. After tucking one of the sonogram images into his wallet, the rest into her small backpack, and after she relieved her screaming bladder, they'd headed out of Baldwin and back towards Shadow Valley on his sled.

Linc got one of the prospects to cover his shift at the bar so he could take her to dinner. They found a little diner off the beaten path, which had great homemade food. Once her stomach was full, they headed out again on a long ride while the sun started to set.

It felt great to wrap her arms around Linc, press her cheek into his cut and hold him tight. The child she was scared she lost earlier in the day tucked between them. On the straightaways, Linc drove his bike with one hand on the throttle and one hand on her thigh, his fingers squeezing it every once in a while.

She loved being on the back of Linc's bike, she loved hanging on to him. She felt safe with him. It was shocking to think she felt just as safe with the biker in front of her as she did with her police office father and brother. Maybe more.

Once the sun was just about down, he pulled into a parking lot of a small store in Shadow Valley, one she had never paid attention to before. Mostly because she never had a reason.

Mommy and Munchkin.

Even though it was getting dark out, the lights still burned bright through the storefront.

He shut down his sled, kicked the stand down and assisted her off the bike.

"Why are we here? It's late, Linc. They're probably ready to close."

"Called 'em when you were in the bathroom at the diner. Asked the owner if he could stay for a little bit."

Jayde arched a brow. "Really?"

"Yeah. Said it was important."

Jayde rolled her eyes. "You heard what the tech said, we have twenty-nine weeks to do things like this. There was no reason to make them stay late."

Linc shrugged then dismounted, wrapping his arm over her shoulders. He leaned down and pressed his lips to her temple. "Baby, he didn't mind when I told him we're having our first kid."

First kid.

She opened her mouth, but nothing escaped. Without waiting for her response, Linc was steering her through the front door anyway.

The owner greeted them immediately and gave them his congratulations.

"You said you need a crib." He swept his hand toward one corner of the locally owned baby store. "As you see we have a nice selection. We even have a few used cribs, if you're interested."

Cribs? Her head twisted toward Linc. "We're here for a crib? Already? Linc..."

Linc squeeze her shoulders, ignoring her surprise. "Want the safest one you got," he told the older gentleman. "Don't care how much it is, as long as it's safe. You said you got lay-away, right?"

The owner's smile widened. "We do. That's not a problem. And once it's paid for, we even deliver it and set it up for you."

Linc gave him a nod.

"We don't even have a place yet," Jayde murmured. They certainly couldn't set it up in Linc's room above church, and a crib being delivered to her parents' house would be a huge red flag.

Huge.

The shop owner turned his warm brown eyes on her. "That's not a problem. We can hold it until you're ready. We try to accommodate everyone as best as we can. We really appreciate it when folks shop local instead of at the big box stores. Come this way."

Linc dropped his arms from her shoulders and reached for his wallet. While Jayde stood in place, Linc walked with the man toward the display of cribs. She blinked as she watched him pull out the sonogram image from where he tucked it away to show the owner, who patted him on the back and congratulated him again.

She shook herself mentally and wandered over to where they were talking. She was in no rush, though, since it sounded like Linc was asking all the right questions.

But as she headed in that direction, her heart began to race, and a little bit of panic began to set in.

Hearing the heartbeat, seeing the baby on the monitor, the sonogram pictures, and now the crib...

Holy shit, she was going to become someone's mother.

She was going to be responsible for another human being.

Their lives would never be the same again.

CHAPTER SEVEN

"Grandchildren are *such* a blessing," April said in a sing-song voice as she carried Zeke around the dinner table over to Mitch.

Jayde watched her father's expression, which was already closed off, turn darker, as he stared at his grandson.

Zak sat at the other end of the table, his jaw tight, his expression just as hard.

This was not going well. At all.

Whoever thought this was a good idea needed to be slapped. She turned her head toward Axel and lifted her brows at him, giving him a *good-fucking-job-asshole* look.

Axel shot her a frown and then ignored her, turning his gaze back to their brooding father.

Clearly, Mitch Jamison was never going to accept having a biker in his family. At least one that wasn't a Blue Avenger like him and Axel, the law enforcement MC they belonged to. But a non-cop MC? Never.

If he couldn't soften up and accept Z, his own son, back into his life, how was he ever going to accept Linc?

He wasn't.

Jayde flattened a hand against her belly as it churned. Having this dinner was a complete mistake. It was only going to make things worse.

Her gaze bounced from one uneaten plate to the next. No one at that table ate more than a forkful of her mother's *to-die-for* meatloaf and creamy smashed potatoes with her famous brown gravy. Food that normally would have been scarfed down in seconds.

Her father's chair legs squealed as he pushed away from the table with a shove, but before he could stand, her mother plopped Baby Z right into his lap. He had no choice but to grab Zeke, or the kid would've tumbled to the ground. Facing his grandfather with his feet planted on his thighs, Zeke fell forward with a happy squeal and wrapped his arms tightly around her father's neck. "Pop-pop!"

What?

Around the table, everyone froze. Her dad had spent zero time with Zeke since he was born. How did the baby even know who he was or what to call him?

All eyes turned to Sophie who was sitting quietly to Zak's right, a small smile curving her lips as she stared down at her plate.

Jayde's gaze slid back to her father, who was staring at Zeke, their faces inches apart. If her father broke down right then and there, Jayde was going to curl up under the table and start bawling.

Her dad cleared his throat. Then cleared it even harder the second time and said, "That's right... I'm your pop-pop, Zeke."

"Zee!" Baby Z screamed, then laughed. And without warning gave his pop-pop a big sloppy kiss on the chin.

Her father cleared his throat again and closed his eyes, avoiding them all.

Jayde glanced at Axel, who was staring blankly at a spot somewhere over their father's shoulder. Bella was swiping at her face with her palms. April had her hands over her mouth, a stray tear running down her cheek. Sophie was now watching Zeke in her father-in-law's arms with a huge, satisfied smile on her face and tears in her eyes.

Jayde finally turned to smile at Zak.

Who was gone.

How the hell did he sneak away from the table without anyone knowing?

Sophie's gaze landed on Z's empty chair and she frowned. She pulled her napkin from her lap, threw it on the table and went to get up.

Jayde gave her a quick shake of the head and hurried from the table in the only direction Z could have went without anyone noticing.

The foyer outside the dining room was empty, so she hooked a left and ran up the stairs to the second floor, only to find the hallway empty, too. She rushed down the hall and found her brother in his old room.

His old room that was now their father's office. A room that no longer even hinted that it was once Z's childhood bedroom. As soon as Zak had moved out of the house and into church when he became a prospect, their father threw out everything in that room. Trophies, comic books, action figures, posters, his furniture, any clothes left behind. Anything and everything that had been Zak's.

Every picture in the house that had included Z had been changed out.

Even the lines drawn on the wall in the pantry measuring their growth throughout their childhood had been painted over.

Nothing was left.

"Had to wipe every fuckin' trace of me from this house," Z said, standing in the middle of the room, staring at the large desk near the window that held a desktop computer. "Every fuckin' trace. Not one picture. Not one fuckin' memory."

Jayde wanted to say something that would make him feel better, but she had no idea what, because what he was saying was the truth. And she was sure it killed her older brother to be wiped clean so easily from his family's home and life.

"Mom..." he said, his voice thick.

"Mom didn't agree with any of it."

He shook his head, not meeting her eyes. "Still allowed it."

And that was very true, too. "Yes, she did. You know she was always one to try to keep the peace."

"Shoulda stood up to 'im."

"She has to live with him." Even though Jayde agreed with what he said, she still felt the need to defend their mother.

No matter how her father felt about her brother, she knew he loved her mom fiercely and completely.

"Gonna be able to live with it when he wipes your ass clean from this house, too?" He turned and pinned his blue eyes on her. He was trying to mask the hurt in them, but he couldn't. That wound went way too deep.

Her heart squeezed. "Downstairs... He took a step forward, Z."

"Only 'cause he was forced to. Mom gave 'im no choice but to take my son." Z's fingers curled into tight fists and a muscle ticked in his jaw. "*My fuckin' son*. Hates me so fuckin' much that he didn't even want to hold my son! *His grandson!*"

Jayde winced at the agony in her brother's words. That pain cut her deep, too. There was nothing more that she wanted than her family to be whole again. It had been broken for way too long.

Axel was slowly coming around. Her brothers' relationship had improved in the last couple of years thanks to Bella, Sophie and Zeke's birth. But it was still nowhere where it needed to be.

"This dinner was supposed to help mend your relationship with Dad, Z. Or at least be the start of it. Pulling this bullshit by leaving the table when there was an actual breakthrough isn't going to help."

Z's eyes narrowed on her. "The only reason you wanted this was to save your own fuckin' ass, Jayde. I know it, you know it. Tryin' to soften the blow that Mitch is gonna feel when you tell 'im you're fuckin' knocked up. With a fuckin' biker, no less. Usin' me an' my son for your own gain."

Jayde sucked in a sharp breath. "This was Axel's idea, but you agreed to it."

"Yeah, I fuckin' did. Tryin' to help you out. Help Linc. Shouldn't've though. Big fuckin' mistake." He raked a hand through his dark hair. "Fuck!"

"Why is it a mistake? Because you actually felt something deep down when you saw Dad holding your son? Realized that he's still your father and Zeke's grandfather, no matter what? That for good or bad, he's still blood? Zeke has no clue about the past. None. He's the innocent in all of this. Your son has no idea you went to prison and why. He has no idea how Dad, and even Axel, condemned you for it. Now's the time to mend those fucking fences before he learns about all of that. It's time to put all of that in the past."

"My son's DAMC born an' bred. He's got more than enough fuckin' family," Zak muttered.

"Be the fucking bigger man, Zak. Please. Be the bigger man. This will help all of us."

"It'll help you, Jayde. That's it. You. Don't need his judgmental ass in my fuckin' life. You do."

"And that's where you're wrong. I know he's done you ugly. We *all* know that. But do you really want Zeke to not have any grandparents in his life? Sophie's family disowned her. Wants nothing to do with her. For what? Simply because you're a biker, Z. She married and had a kid with a biker against their wishes. Do you want that to continue here, too? With all of us? Do I want my baby to never know his or her grandparents, either? No! I don't know shit about Linc's family. Not one thing. Mom and Dad may be the only grandparents this baby will ever have!" She stepped closer to her brother, who was now staring at his boots, his hands on his hips. "We *need* to make this work. *Please.*"

Z lifted his head, tilted it and studied Jayde. "This is all 'cause Linc knocked you the fuck up."

"It wasn't his fault," Jayde murmured.

"Bullshit."

Jayde shook her head. "It was mine. At Hawk's wedding... I... I knew he'd been drinking and his guard was down..."

"Bullshit, Jayde. He's been chasin' your tail for a while."

Jayde winced at being called *tail*. "But I took that last step. I pushed him when he was weak. Don't blame him. Blame me."

"Yeah, well, that man downstairs is gonna go fuckin' ballistic an' he ain't gonna hear that excuse. He's gonna blame Linc no matter what you fuckin' say."

"I know," she said softly. "And this is why it's important that he accepts the DAMC." She slapped a hand to her forehead and sighed loudly. "Why does he have to be so damn stubborn?"

Z stepped toe to toe with her, and got in her face, growling, "Because his father was fuckin' killed by a rival MC, Jayde, that's why. He don't wanna admit how hard that hit 'im, but it fuckin' did. An' not only that, his only fuckin' brother landed in prison. Doin' life for murderin' some of those fuckers. He lost his older brother an' his father all 'cause of the DAMC. If it wasn't for the club..." Z shook his head. "Why I tried so hard to change this fuckin' club. Turn the fuckin' tables. Worked so hard, only to end up in fuckin' prison myself." Z spun away from her and strode to the window to stare out. "Fuckin' disappointed 'im."

"He probably thought he'd lose you the same way. I'm sure it freaked him out. And when you went to prison like Rocky, his nightmare became true."

"Yeah," Z grunted. "You an' Axel weren't born yet when Bear was killed. When Rocky was arrested, convicted, sent away. Jayde, you weren't around to hear 'im break down behind his bedroom door." Zak pressed his forehead to the window. "I fuckin' heard it. Shouldn't remember it, but I do. It fuckin' killed him. *Killed him*. An' then I went against 'im an' followed in their footsteps. *Jesus fuck*." The last came out as a tortured whisper.

Jayde's breath hitched, and she whispered, "Would you do it differently if you could?"

She watched her brother's shoulders rise and fall as he inhaled a deep breath.

"What do you think?" he asked her.

Her instinct would be to say yes, since no one would want to do ten years in SCI Fayette for a crime they didn't commit. Hell, no one wanted to do ten years in a small cell for a crime they *did* commit. "Yes."

So when Z turned from the window, his answer shocked the hell out of her. "You'd be wrong. Would do it all over in a split fuckin' second. Know why, Jayde?" He pointed down at the floor. "That fuckin' woman downstairs. She's my fuckin' everything. If I hadn't patched into the DAMC, never woulda went to prison. Never went to prison, never woulda had a homecomin' party that night. If there was no party, then never woulda made the best mistake of my fuckin' life. Mighta never met Sophie. She gave me my life back. Gave me my son. Owe her everything."

Jayde blinked back the burn in her eyes. When she went back downstairs, she was giving Sophie a hug. That was for damn sure. "You fought so hard for her."

"Damn fuckin' straight. Now I do it all for the two of 'em."

Jayde could only hope Linc would fight that hard for her. For them. She wanted that kind of love and dedication. That passion and loyalty. And she didn't see it just between Zak and Sophie. She saw it between Axel and Bella. Axel had fought just as hard for Bella.

Neither of her brothers ever gave up when it came to claiming their women. Making them theirs.

Jesus, to have that deep desire and need for another person like that... And then to go balls to the wall until you got want you wanted...

Well, it had to run deep in the Jamison veins, since she never gave up and she finally got what she wanted when she had chased Linc down that night. Her hand dropped to her belly. Though she got a little unexpected surprise along with it.

She had hoped tonight would help pave the way for breaking the news to her parents. It needed to be soon since the time was approaching when she'd no longer be able to hide it with baggy shirts. But of course, she should have known the Jamisons were too damn stubborn to make anything easy.

"I don't know what I'm going to do, Z," Jayde finally said in a broken whisper.

"Nothin' tonight. Gonna get Linc set up in a place, 'cause you know your ass is gonna get kicked out. Even if you don't tell 'em, ain't gonna be able to hide it for much longer."

"Yeah."

"It's about time you get out on your own. Make your own decisions."

"Zak... Do you think Linc will make a good father?" She thought back on the day of the ultrasound and his face when he saw their baby on the big screen. How he tucked one of the images into his wallet.

"No fuckin' clue, but won't know 'til you give 'im a chance. An' maybe he's wonderin' if you'll make a good mother."

Jayde snorted, then punched Z in the arm. "Never thought of that, asshole."

Z smirked. "Know it. But it's true. Not all women are good mothers."

"We were lucky."

"True. But we'd be luckier if Mom wasn't stuck with that stubborn fucker."

"Dad loves Mom just as much as you love Sophie."

Z sighed. "Yeah."

"Can't blame her for sticking."

"Right."

"So now what?"

"Goin' downstairs, grabbin' my woman an' my son, an' gettin' the fuck outta here."

"Mom would be happier if you stayed and finished dinner."

"Yeah, sucks not eatin' her meatloaf. Sophie needs that recipe. But don't think I can sit at that table any longer. Not tonight."

"We need to figure out a way to fix this."

Z shook his head. "Not sure it's possible, sis."

"I think Zeke is the key."

"Yeah. Maybe. Soph can bring 'im by when I ain't here. Let 'im visit with his grandparents. Soften up that stubborn fuck."

Jayde snorted. Like father, like son. Poor Zeke was doomed to be just as stubborn. "He hears you calling him that, he's never going to soften up."

Z shrugged and headed toward the door. "No loss."

Jayde wished Zak didn't feel that way. Z paused in the doorway and looked over his shoulder. "Gonna get Linc to move outta church this week an' into a place, even if temporary. Then it's up to you to break the news."

"Can I wait until I'm showing?"

Shaking his head, Z's eyes dropped to her stomach and the loose shirt she was wearing. "Do whatcha gotta do, sis, but ain't gonna be able to hide it much longer." He started to step out into the hallway, but stopped. "Hey..."

"Yeah?"

"Was a good idea. Smart."

Her brows furrowed. "What was?"

"Considerin' Bella an' Ax to take your kid." With that, he turned and headed down the hallway with the swagger that only her brother could make look cool.

Her head snapped up when she heard the rumble of straight pipes approaching the house.

Now, who the hell could that be?

L inc shut his sled down and yanked the black skull bandana off the lower half of his face, then slipped his sunglasses into the neck of his T-shirt. He stared at the typical two-story home, in the typical middle-class neighborhood. Typical two-car garage. Typical manicured lawn, most likely with a sprinkler system. Typical wooden rocking chairs sitting on the front porch. It was probably where Mitch and April drank their morning coffee, read the paper and chit-chatted about their plans for the day.

Typical middle-class family.

Sophie's car sat in the paved driveway. So did Axel's custom

Harley. The one the pig paid his cousin, Jag, a lot of money to build for him.

Compared to Axel's bike, the one that sat between Linc's legs looked like a junkyard special. Yeah, it ran great, but it wasn't custom, nor was it even shiny with chrome. The sled got him from point A to point B. And it had no problem keeping up with the pack during club runs.

He hoped to save up money to get something bigger, better, more badass. But now that Jayde was carrying his kid, that dream was all shot to shit. All his money would go to raising his kid from here on out. Providing for Jayde. Making sure she finished her law degree. Doing whatever he had to do to make sure she didn't end up hating his ass for taking away her dreams.

Yeah, Z had said the club would help and there's no way Linc could turn that down, but he wanted to do what he could on his own. It was a sense of pride more than anything.

He was swinging his leg over the sled when the front door of the house opened and the Jamison brothers walked out, with Z carrying Zeke. Sophie and Bella followed closely behind.

And everyone's eyes were on him.

Hard to be stealthy when running straight exhaust pipes on a hog.

He stood next to his sled and steeled himself, since Axel was heading directly toward him. "What are you doing here?"

"Someone forgot my fuckin' invitation," Linc grumbled.

"You weren't invited," Axel stated.

"Was a reason for that, brother," Z added.

"Why? So you all could make decisions for my woman and my kid without me?"

"*Your woman?*" Axel repeated, his eyebrows raised as high as the American flag that hung from the front porch.

"Axel," Bella murmured, stepping up to her ol' man and placing a hand on his arm. "Clearly he wants to do the right thing."

"Right thing would've been not to knock up my sister," Axel

grumbled in a low voice. He turned to glance over his shoulder at the house. "Speaking of which, here she comes."

With wide eyes, Jayde rushed down the steps of the porch and over to where they were standing in the driveway. "What are you doing here?" she whispered fiercely, her eyes bouncing from Linc and back to the house like a tennis match.

"Don't want you to do this on your own, Jayde. Here to stand by your side and take whatever shit your father's gonna shovel in our direction."

She opened her mouth to respond, but Mitch Jamison running down the stairs and heading in their direction made her snap her jaw shut and turn a whiter shade of pale.

Blue eyes, just like Jayde's, were narrowed dangerously on him. "What the hell are you doing here? Zak, take your club business elsewhere. Not in front of my house."

A slim, but curvy, pretty brown-haired woman, who Linc could only guess was Jayde's mother, followed on his heels, a worried look on her face. "Mitch."

Mitch ignored his wife.

Z handed Zeke over to Sophie. "Babe, take 'im an' get in the car."

"Zak..."

"Babe, no lip. Get gone." With a frown, Sophie headed in that direction, but very slowly. Z shot her an impatient look, but turned to face his father. "Don't want your neighbors findin' out your true roots?" Z said, shaking his head and crossing his arms over his chest. He rolled back on his heels. "'Fraid they're gonna find out where you came from? What kind of biker trash runs through your 5-0 veins?"

"Z," Axel started.

Z lifted his hand and glanced at him. "Brother, we've been doin' all right lately, don't fuck that shit up."

Bella put an arm around Axel's waist and gave it a squeeze. "He's right, honey. Stay out of it."

"It's my sister," Axel muttered.

Mitch's spine snapped straight. "This about Jayde?" His eyes narrowed on Linc. "You're here about my daughter?"

Now was as good a time as any to state his case before things went deeper into the shitter. "Know you don't like bikers. Know you don't want Jayde to have anything to do with DAMC..."

"Linc," Jayde whispered, reaching for him.

He needed to get what he had to say out before anyone stopped him, including Jayde. "Know you're gonna judge Jayde unfairly about havin' my kid."

"Linc," Jayde squeaked.

"Fuck," Z muttered.

"Holy shit," Axel groaned.

"Oh no," Bella breathed.

Linc's gaze slid from the thunderous look on Mitch's face, the shocked look on her mother's face, to his president, who had his head hanging and was shaking it, to Jayde.

Her eyes were squeezed shut when she groaned, "He didn't know."

What? "What?" *Oh fuck.*

"He didn't fucking know, Linc! I didn't tell him yet." She waved a hand between the two of them. "We haven't even had a chance to settle things between us yet. I wasn't planning on telling him until we at least had a place."

"Fuck," Linc muttered, this time out loud.

Color rushed into her cheeks and she shouted, "Yeah, fuck! This dinner was a start at trying to get the family back together again. To fix things before I told them."

"You didn't tell 'em?"

"This dinner wasn't to announce your fucking news!" Axel shouted.

"This is a joke, right? I'm being pranked?" Mitch's head swiveled back and forth as he searched the yard. "There better be fucking cameras hidden in the bushes and we're all going to have a big fucking laugh after this... *Right?*" Mitch spun toward Axel. "Please tell me they're pulling one over on me and you're in on this..." His gaze swung from Axel to Jayde, hesitated for a split second before swinging toward Linc. "Because if it isn't..."

"Honey," Jayde's mother whispered, grabbing onto her husband's arm. He jerked out of her grasp when he took a heavy step forward.

Shit.

The man's face was turning an ugly shade of purple. "What the fuck did you do?"

"Daddy..." Jayde started, but her father swatted a hand in her direction.

"What did you fucking do?" Mitch roared, taking another step closer to Linc.

Linc tipped his head from his left shoulder to his right and loosened his body, as he fisted his hands, getting prepared for a fight he didn't want to have.

Especially with the grandfather of his unborn kid, who happened to be a fucking *cop*.

Mitch's head snapped toward Jayde. "He rape you?"

A collective female gasp rose up and Jayde rushed forward to step between Linc and Mitch, her palms up. "Dad, no! He didn't rape me. Holy shit."

His dark blue eyes dropped to his daughter. "You wanted to have sex with... with... *him?*"

Linc doubted the color in Jayde's cheeks was from anger now.

"I—I..." she stuttered.

Mitch glared at Linc. "*You* were the one I caught her with that night... that night when the bar got shot up. You've been preying on her all this time?"

"No!" Jayde shouted.

Zak grabbed Jayde's arm and pulled her back behind Linc.

"Brother, get the fuck outta here," Z told him through gritted teeth. "Take 'er an' go."

Mitch pointed at Zak. "This is all your fucking fault, Zackary! You're nothing but a bad seed. It's your fault that she was anywhere near this... this... *guy*." He spun toward Axel. "And you! Your sister thinks this shit's acceptable because of you being with *her*." He jabbed a finger toward Bella. "I fought hard to keep my children out of that life. To protect you, like a good father should. But you all... you all... just shit all over everything I've fought for."

"Mitch," Jayde's mother whispered again, clamping a hand on his forearm. Her words were shaky when she begged, "Don't do this."

His gaze dropped to his wife. "Did you know about this?"

"No, I had no idea."

Z murmured to Linc. "Take 'er an' get gone, Linc. Now. Takin' Soph an' Zeke home. Gettin' the fuck outta here. But ain't leavin' until you two do."

"No!" Mitch shouted. "You're not taking her anywhere." He took another step toward Linc and Jayde. Axel stepped between them, and Z's body went tight next to Linc. "She's not going anywhere. *We'll* deal with whatever mess she's in."

By "we'll" Linc was pretty fucking sure the man didn't mean all of them. And the cop was not going to make any decisions for his future kid.

"Listen to your prez an' get the fuck outta here. *Now,*" Z muttered under his breath. "Gonna end up with a fuckin' bullet where you don't want one if you don't."

"Get inside," Mitch ordered Jayde, swinging his arm toward the house behind him.

Fuck that. Z was right. It was time to shut this thing down. "Get on my sled, Jayde."

Jayde's head swung between Linc and her father. "But—"

Linc snagged her arm and pushed her gently toward his bike. He continued to face her angry father. The fuck if he was turning his back on the man. "Get on my fuckin' sled, Jayde."

"If you get on his bike, Jayde... If you leave with him, don't ever come the hell home. Do you hear me?"

"Mitch!" Jayde's mother cried out.

Mitch pointed at Linc. "You leave with him, Jayde. You don't come back."

"Please, baby, get on my sled," Linc said softly as he spotted the tears running down her cheeks, a confused look on her face. She was torn.

He didn't blame her.

It wasn't supposed to happen this way. Fuck, none of this was supposed to happen at all.

Once again, he fucked up.

"April, get your daughter." Mitch shook his head. "You don't want me touching her right now."

"Dad!" Axel yelled at his father, then turned toward Jayde. "You need to decide what you're doing right now. You're either going inside with Mom and Dad, or you're leaving with Linc. Choose now and get going."

"Better think long and hard on that, Jayde," Mitch warned. "Already made one mistake. Don't make another."

"Don't do this, Dad! Don't make me choose."

Jesus. The agony in Jayde's voice twisted Linc's gut.

Mitch threw his hands up, spun on his heels and tossed over his shoulder, "You already chose when you allowed him between your legs. Never thought my only daughter would end up being trash."

A muscle popped in Linc's jaw as he surged forward only to be snagged by the arm by Z, and Axel rushed to plant two hands on his chest, holding him back.

Axel shook his head. "Ain't smart. Right now, shit's fixable. You fucking get into it with him, you do some damage, it might not be. His fucking pride is hurt right now. He'll eventually see reason."

Linc looked over Axel's shoulder when the front door slammed shut.

"I know what you're seeing in him right now, and I recognize that it's ugly. Real fucking ugly. I'm not liking what I'm seeing, either. He's not only my father, but I have to work with him. He's my fucking supervisor." Axel sucked in a breath. "No matter what an asshole he's being right now, know that he loves Jayde." Axel looked at Z, who still had a tight hold on Linc. "He loves you, too, whether you realize it or not. Hate to say this about my father because he's a proud man, but he's scared. Deep down he's fucking terrified that he's going to lose his family to the shit the club deals with. Just like Granddad. Just like Rocky. He doesn't want to let his guard down because if he does... and then something happens to any one of you..." Axel shook his head. "I don't think he'll recover."

"Got a dick way of showin' us he loves us, Axel. Totally fuckin' dick," Z grumbled, finally releasing Linc's arm.

Axel dropped his hands from Linc's chest and stepped back. "Can't argue with that." He turned toward Jayde, who had Bella's arms wrapped tightly around her. "Looks like Dad made your choice for you, sis. You can come stay with us if you want until things get settled."

"No," Linc said, shaking his head. "No. She ain't going anywhere but with me, got me?"

"My car. My clothes. Everything..." Jayde whispered, still staring at the house.

"Doubt your gonna see that shit for a long time, if ever," Z muttered. "Likes to hold a fuckin' grudge."

"I'll talk to him," Axel said.

"Just make sure he doesn't get rid of anything. Please."

Axel nodded. "I'll do my best. We're getting out of here. I'm taking Bella home. We've had enough fun this evening, I don't think I can take any more." He faced Zak. "You good here?"

"We're bailin', too."

Bella and Jayde gave each other a look of surprise when the two brothers clasped hands and bumped shoulders before moving apart. Axel escorted Bella to his sled, while Z stood eyeballing Linc.

"Get gone, Linc. Take 'er either to the Motor Inn or church for the night. We'll figure this shit out first thing in the mornin' at church. Time's run out. I'll text you."

Linc swallowed hard and nodded. His gaze slid to Jayde, who was still staring at the house, her eyes red, her expression wrecked.

Fuck. He did that. He put that look on her face. He fucked up her life all because he couldn't keep up the good fight and resist her anymore.

Couldn't keep his dick in his pants.

"Got enough scratch?"

His president's voice pulled him out of his thoughts. "Yeah."

"Not leavin' 'til you're clear from here. So get gone."

Linc watched Z move toward Sophie's car where his family was waiting.

"Brother!" Linc yelled out.

Z stopped but didn't turn around.

"Thanks."

"Don't thank me yet," Z tossed over his shoulder.

CHAPTER EIGHT

Linc's arms encircled Jayde as they lay still dressed on top of the sheets. Jayde's shoes were somewhere across the room where she whipped them in frustration as soon as they had entered the room at Shadow Valley Motor Inn.

He couldn't get the image out of his mind of her dropping hard to her knees in the middle of the room before curling into herself, sobbing so hard her body was wracked with them.

He had picked her up, put her on the bed, and, after shucking his boots and cut, had joined her, keeping a tight hold of her as she soaked his T-shirt with hot tears. Neither of them said a word. He figured he'd keep his mouth shut and let her work out whatever was in her head first, without her needing his most likely unwanted opinion.

Eventually her body relaxed, she nuzzled her cheek tighter against his chest, and her breathing leveled out. He couldn't see her face because her hair was covering it, but he had to assume she had finally fallen asleep.

He laid there for hours, staring up at the ceiling, trying to make a plan for their future.

He hadn't wanted an ol' lady. Not yet, anyway. *Fuck*, he certainly hadn't wanted a kid. But sometimes life didn't go as planned.

Problem was, he kept finding that out the hard way.

While growing up, he'd learned things were never as easy as they seemed. Like Jayde, he hadn't wanted for anything growing up. His parents spoiled the fuck out of him. They were proud of him. His grades, his after-school activities. His football and wrestling throughout junior and senior high school. Hell, he was so good when it came to wrestling, he'd made it to Regionals, then the State Championships, even on to Nationals a couple times. He was good. So good, college recruiters scouted him as a junior. Colleges kept in communication with his father. They were making plans...

His future was set.

Or so he thought...

When Jayde shifted in his arms, he swept her long, dark hair out of her face and peered down into her blue eyes. She was awake.

Snuggling closer, her arm tightened around his waist and she blinked up at him.

"Sorry 'bout all this shit, baby. Told you I was gonna fuck up." Hell, that was a given.

"I just didn't expect it to be this soon."

"Yeah," he breathed. "Shoulda believed me."

She turned her face into his chest and laughed.

He grinned down at her, combing his fingers through her hair. "Tell me what you want, Jayde."

She tipped her blue eyes to his. He was glad to see that they were clear and focused, unlike earlier. "Though I'm scared that we're not ready... this baby."

"Yeah, I'm scared, too. No matter what, we're having this kid. What else?"

Her chin dug into his chest as she stared up at him. "What do you mean?"

"Gotta meet with Z in the morning. *We're* decidin' what the fuck's gonna go on from here. No one else is decidin' but me and you. So, need to get shit straight. What do you want, Jayde? From me. For us."

Her gaze slid to the side before coming back to meet his. "I want us to be happy."

What felt like a thick band tightened around his chest, almost as if the breath was being squeezed out of him. "Can't promise you that."

"Why not?"

"Because shit happens, Jayde. Can think you got shit under control, heading in the direction things need to be, and then..."

"Then?"

"Shit happens," he repeated.

"Like this baby."

"Right. But the baby's a given. So, where do you wanna go from here? Got our jobs, but no place to live."

"I don't have anything but that job right now. I don't have a car, clothes, nothing."

"Right. Gonna hafta take care of that."

"I don't make that much money working for Kiki. I do okay, but not enough to get a place, buy a new wardrobe. Buy a car."

It killed him that her voice got shaky at the end. "Gonna get a loaner from Crash. That'll solve that."

"He has clunkers!"

"Yeah, and long as it gets you from here to there, that's all you fuckin' need. Don't need no fancy-ass yellow Camaro. Need something safe. We'll get something better later. Right now, you just need wheels."

"Shit," she grumbled. "Apparently, I need a place, too."

"*We* need a place," he corrected her.

She lifted her head. "Are you sure you're ready to live together? We had sex twice. We only had one actual 'date,' Linc, and that was after the ultrasound to buy a crib for a baby. I'm not sure that either of us is ready for that."

The doubt in her words ate at him. When she had first walked into The Iron Horse and told him she was pregnant, none of that had been in her voice. None. So he ignored it, since he didn't want to feed into it. He needed her to be sure that he wanted to be with her. Wanted this kid. "Diesel's talking 'bout moving out to the farm. Maybe Ace will let us move above the pawn shop for now. Just a place to settle 'til we can find something better."

"Linc..."

He grabbed her chin and tilted her face toward him. "Don't wanna live with me?"

"That place has one bedroom."

"Yeah."

"One bathroom."

"Yeah."

"That's close quarters for two people who were not together to suddenly live in the same place."

"Yeah, baby... Listen... Been wanting you for a long time. Had this discussion already—"

"You were avoiding me."

"No, was having a hard time resisting you. Knew if I did what I wanted to do, if I took what I wanted, it was gonna cause problems. And tonight proved I was right."

When she opened her mouth, he lifted a hand to stop her.

"Gotta remember your oldest brother's my prez, baby. He calls the shots. Your other brother's a fuckin' cop. Your *father's* a cop. I ain't stupid. Got men watching over you that I didn't wanna fuck with. The only one scarier than those three combined is Diesel. I might be good with my fists, but taking on the men in your family is just plain stupid."

"Zak took it well. Axel, too." She brushed her fingers over the area where he had sported a bruise from Axel's punch. At least that had finally faded into oblivion. "Eventually."

"Thank fuck for Bella. 'Cause if Bella hadn't softened Axel the fuck up over Z and the club in general, have a feeling I'd be being buried 'bout now."

"They forget I'm twenty-eight. They still see me as sixteen."

"Right. Still their baby sister. Still daddy's lil girl."

She sighed.

"Nothing wrong with that. Means they care 'bout you, being protective."

"I doubt my father's seeing me as his little girl right about now."

"Hoping Axel's right and he gets over it. Kids need their grand-parents." He winced. *Fuck*. He stupidly just opened the door to a subject he didn't want to discuss.

And just like he suspected she'd do, she headed in that direction. "Speaking of, what about—"

He twisted until she was beneath him and he was staring directly into those baby blues of hers. "Baby, thinking we need to sleep now. You need rest."

Her eyes narrowed on him. "But you said you wanted to figure things out before meeting with Z."

That was true, he did say that. But now he didn't want to open a can of worms. One he wouldn't be able to put the lid back on. "Yeah, can do that in the morning. Now we need to sleep."

"I already slept some, I'm no longer tired."

"Gonna tire you out. Then you'll sleep."

Her eyebrows shot up. "Oh? You think I want to have sex with you?"

"Don't think it, know it."

Her lips twitched.

"Tempted the fuck outta me. Hunted me down 'til you got my dick. Now you got it, can't get enough of it."

Jayde snorted. "You think?"

"Yeah." He slipped his hands down her arms until their fingers intertwined, then he lifted them up over her head and pressed them into the mattress. "Gotta get you naked. Wanna see that body of yours."

She frowned. "The body that's changing?"

"Nothing wrong with that."

"Uh huh, tell me that again when I'm as stretched and miserable as Jewel was with Violet."

"No matter how big she got, that woman was still fuckin' beautiful. She was growing D's daughter inside her. Now, too much talking, not enough fuckin'."

Jayde pinned her lips together and rolled her eyes before saying, "Waiting on you since you're on top."

"Yeah," he breathed. She was waiting on him. He had no problem getting things started.

He wanted to apologize again right then and there for fucking up her life. For making things difficult for her. Especially with her parents. But apologizing wasn't going to change their circumstances.

"Now I got you in my bed, not letting you out."

She arched a brow. "Never?"

He dropped his head until his lips were right above hers. "Nope."

"That might get a little inconvenient."

"Yep." He traced her plump bottom lip with the tip of his tongue. He nibbled along it, inhaling her warm breath as he did so. It hitched, and she shifted beneath him until his dick was lined up along her soft heat. That heat he wanted to sink deep into. Remind her who she now belonged to.

They needed to get naked, but he was in no rush. He didn't have to worry about her going anywhere. She had nowhere to go. Without even meaning to, he had made her his.

Yeah, he'd been panicked at first at the news. But now... Now, seeing her in his bed, or more like the motel's bed, made him realize how much he had actually wanted her. The relief at now having her. For a long time, he'd been worried some other man would come along and he'd have to watch her get claimed by someone else. While it was difficult keeping his distance, it would have been even more torturous watching her with another man for the rest of his fucking life.

Now there was no risk of that. No risk of someone coming and stealing Jayde away.

Though the fucking situation wasn't ideal, they'd make the best of it. Hell, they had no choice but to do just that.

And right now, he wanted to make the best of the current situation. Which was her being beneath him in this bed.

He stretched their entangled hands up over her head and took her mouth until she was squirming under him, making those sweet fucking sounds she made when she was getting worked up.

He did that to her. He could make her react like that. Even that first night with his belly full of whiskey, it had been good between him. Which had made it even harder to walk away afterward.

Almost impossible.

But after she had made him lose his mind, his sense had slowly returned. Reality had set in, washed over him.

However, now... now he had his president's blessing. Or so it seemed. And Linc hoped to hell he was right. Hoped like fuck that Z didn't change his mind and then tomorrow tell him to stay away from his sister.

Because that shit wasn't going to fly with him. Not at all.

He pressed his lips to Jayde's ear. "Gonna give you my dick. Want it?"

Jayde's answer was her hips lifting off the bed to grind against his erection.

Yeah, she wanted it.

He sucked on her earlobe, then traced his tongue down the beating pulse in her neck to the hollow of her throat. He sucked the skin there and her moan vibrated against his lips.

Freeing one of his hands, he found where her shirt met her jeans and slipped his hand underneath it. He spread his fingers over the smooth, warm skin of her belly. A piece of him was inside of her. Her body protected and nourished something that belonged to him. A child who would carry on the Lincoln family name.

His heart thumped heavily in his chest as he tried to imagine what his son or daughter would look like. In real life. In actual 3D. Not just in a flat black and white image.

He mentally shook himself. Now wasn't the time for that. Now was the time for his woman. For Jayde.

He needed to do right by her. Do his best for her. It was time to stop fucking up.

Her freed hand was clawing at his T-shirt, trying to pull it over his head. But she wasn't getting anywhere with it, not with his weight on her, and she made a frustrated sound.

He lifted his head. "Whataya want, baby? Tell me."

"You know what I want," she said breathlessly, her eyelids heavy, her mouth parted.

The woman was so fucking beautiful that it made his chest ache.

He released her other hand and planted his palms into the mattress, arching his torso away from her.

"Take my shirt off," he demanded, his voice rough.

Grabbing two handfuls of the cotton, she yanked it over his head and tossed it to the side. She scraped her nails down his chest lightly, over his nipples, down his belly, until she got to his belt.

He shook his head. "No. Not yet. Didn't tell you to do that yet."

A grin spread over her face as she stared up at him.

That grin quickly disappeared when he growled, "Unbutton your shirt. *Slowly.*"

Not breaking eye contact, she unbuttoned her pink top, one button at a time with excruciating slowness. And he loved every second of it. The anticipation was driving him fucking nuts. His dick was rock hard in his jeans, his balls aching for release.

"Last time you're wearing that top, got me? Shows way too much of your fuckin' tits. Those are for me and my kid from now on, that's it."

Her eyes widened in surprise for a split second but she quickly hid it. "Do you think you're going to dictate to me now? Let me remind you of something. You haven't claimed me, we aren't living together, we've only had one 'sort of' date. I know the way it is in this club, and I'm used to being around bossy males, but—"

He cut her off. "No buts. If you're gonna be my ol' lady, you gotta listen to your ol' man. That's the way it is. You know that."

"You think you're going to own me." Her voice was flat, controlled.

"Ain't thinking nothing right now 'cept how I'm gonna fuck you. Gonna deal with the rest of that shit later."

"Linc..." she breathed.

"No, baby. Gonna take care of you, protect you, make you my ol' lady, but if you want to get that shit straight right now, then we'll do it right fuckin' now... You're fuckin' mine. Gonna do what I need to do to keep you safe. You gotta listen, got me?" When she didn't answer, he continued, "Also, don't need you fuckin' back-talkin' me in front of your brothers. Hell, in front of my brothers. Ain't gonna be saddled with an ol' lady and a kid and lose my fuckin' balls in the process."

"Saddled?"

Fuck. "Know what I'm sayin'."

"Yes, I do. You got stuck and now think that you're the boss of me."

"Baby, you know how it is."

"I do. And if you think the other women in this club are being bossed around by their men, you haven't been paying attention." He opened his mouth but she shoved her open palm in front of his face, making him jerk his head back in surprise. "No, Linc. You have not been paying attention at all if you think any of your brothers control their ol' ladies. Open your fucking eyes."

"They—"

"No. Think again."

"But—"

"No, you're wrong."

"I—"

"No, Linc, what you think you're seeing isn't actually what's happening."

Bullshit.

He wanted to get laid, not argue. And his dick wasn't liking the way this conversation was going. So, he released a sighed, "Yeah."

Her eyes narrowed, and she frowned. "Are you agreeing with me or throwing in the towel?"

"What will get me laid?"

Her lips rolled inward, and her eyes crinkled at the corner. His dick perked up once again.

He wrapped his fingers around her neck and brushed his thumb back and forth over the soft skin of her delicate throat. "Taking by you not answering, that you want this as much as me."

"I don't know why you'd think that."

He slid his hand down her chest since her shirt was now gaping open, but he stopped right before her bra, which matched the color of her eyes. He wondered if her panties did, too. He'd find out soon enough.

"'Cause your nipples are showing through that bra and are begging for my mouth. Begging for me to pull and twist them."

"They are?" she asked on a hitched breath.

"Yeah, baby, they are."

"I swore you said *too much talking, not enough fuckin'?*"

He crushed his lips to hers, sweeping his tongue through her mouth. He reached between them and unfastened her jeans and before she could push them down, he broke the kiss and flipped her over onto her belly. Straddling her thighs, he yanked her shirt off her arms, unhooked her bra and then jerked her jeans over the round globes of her sweet ass and down her thighs. He tugged them free of her legs and threw them onto the floor along with the matching blue panties.

Figured she'd wear a matching set.

He studied the line of her spine, the two dimples above her ass cheeks, the curves of her hips, her perfectly shaped ass. His hands went to his belt buckle but stilled when she turned her head and looked back at him.

That was when he lost his breath. She peered through her thick dark brown hair at him with those blue eyes of hers, and she just waited for him to take what he wanted.

He could have her. She could be his. And he didn't have to worry anymore. The shit already hit the fan, the cards were already laid out on the table.

Her family had to accept him. Or they wouldn't. But no matter what, he was going nowhere.

He especially wasn't going anywhere right now.

Twisting at her waist, her fingers pulled his away from his buckle and she unfastened it, undid his jeans and whispered, "Anytime now."

His head jerked back then he grinned down at her. "My baby's impatient."

She bucked her ass up beneath him. "Yes, she is."

"My baby wants to be fucked."

A breath hissed out of her. "Yes, she does."

"My baby ain't getting that yet."

She shot him a *what-the-fuck* look, but that only broadened his grin. He shoved his jeans down his thighs and twisted until he could pull them completely off. His jeans landed in a pile on top of hers.

"My baby's getting something else first."

"Well, *your baby* wants you to hurry the hell up."

He snorted, then she squealed when he leaned over and bit her on one of those plump ass cheeks before tossing her onto her back again. Before she could react, he had his shoulders shoved against the backs of her thighs, and his mouth on the sweetest part of her of all.

J ayde's gasp turned into a groan and her fingers dug into the sheets as his hot mouth... and tongue... *oh*, and fingers wreaked havoc.

Holy shit. Holy, holy shit.

Yes, that was worth waiting for. Two of his fingers spread her open as his tongue flicked, his lips sucked. Two more of his fingers curled deep inside her. Her hips danced along with him. She rolled her head back on the pillow with another long, loud groan.

Her fingers crept blindly down until they found his head. For once, she wished his hair was longer, not kept so high and tight like Slade's. Because she wanted to grab handfuls of it to make sure he didn't go *anywhere*.

Oh no. He needed to stay right there. *Right there.*

His teeth scraped her clit, which was swollen and sensitive to his touch.

How'd he get to be so good *at that?*

So fucking good.

The flat of his tongue brushed along her damp folds as he continued to fuck her with his fingers.

His tongue, his fingers, his mouth... *holy crap.*

He lifted his head, but she dug her fingers into his scalp and shoved him back down. "No... not done yet."

Did he just laugh against her pussy?

Who fucking cared! As long as he finished his mission...

She just needed a few more minutes. A few more nips. A few more flicks.

But he gave her more than a few. He worked her harder, faster, more intensely. She squirmed and cried out, her fingers flexing in his hair.

Then... then...

She threw her head back and cried out as her hips shot off the bed, but he still didn't let up. He helped her ride the waves of orgasm until she flopped back down to the bed in a boneless mess.

She couldn't catch her breath; she couldn't think straight. Hell, she didn't want to anyway. She just wanted to lay there and enjoy the euphoria he created.

She blinked up at the stained motel ceiling as it came back into focus and she tipped her head enough to peer down her body at him.

He was still settled between her thighs. His fingers might still be inside her, but his mouth was no longer on her. *Noooo,* instead he wore a huge shiny grin, his green eyes flashing.

"Like that," he stated, because it certainly wasn't a question.

Cocky fuck. "It was okay."

He snorted, pushed up to his hands and knees and moved up her body. "Came like a fuckin' geyser."

She lifted a brow as he came face to face with her. "I did? Huh."

"Flopping around like a fish outta water. Screaming my name."

"I did not."

"Sure fuckin' did."

"Whatever you say."

"That's right, baby, that's the right attitude to have. Whatever I say."

Jayde rolled her eyes, making sure he didn't miss it. "Once again... *Too much talking, not enough fuckin'.*"

He shifted and pressed his cock against her. "Can multi-task. Skilled like that."

"Your mouth should be busy and not with talking," she said, then gasped as he thrusted his hips and entered her with more force than she expected. But once he was inside her, he didn't move.

He closed his eyes and held still. Now he was wearing the expression of euphoria that she was sure had been on her face after she came. He dropped his head, opened his eyes and stared right into hers. "Feel so fuckin' good, baby. So fuckin' tight. So fuckin' hot. *Fuck.*"

He dropped his head farther and sucked one of her nipples into his mouth and he wasn't gentle at all. Then he began to move. He began to do something with his hips that...

Oh, yes.

There was nothing like a man with loose hips. He didn't just move in and out of her, he *rolled* his hips.

Holy shit, it was freaking magical. He couldn't do it when they were in the Camaro. And she certainly didn't remember this hip action during their first time. But then, they hadn't been in a bed that time, either.

But, *wow.*

Sophie always bragged about Zak's loosey-goosey hips, but Jayde ignored that talk because *eww*... Z was her brother. But now she knew what she was gushing on and on about.

Blocking that thought from her head, she dug her heels into Linc's thighs as he pumped smoothly into her like a gentle wave lapping at a lake shore. His mouth went from one nipple to the other, making her arch her back. His tongue circled each nipple, flicked at the hard tip, then he'd suck them deep into his mouth just until she could feel the slight pressure of his teeth against her flesh.

And that was great.

But his movement was way better. Complete strokes. All the way in. All the way out. But every time he drove deep, he'd add a little extra hip action to the end of his thrust.

"Oh, fuck, what are you doing to me?" she cried, throwing her head back and panting. "What are you doing?"

She didn't expect an answer and she didn't get one, because he never lifted his head. Not once. But he did shove his hands underneath her, grabbing her ass and tilting her hips up.

And *oooooh*.

Oh.

Then it hit her at that very moment that they could've been doing this for the past four years. She missed out on this for four freaking years!

She'd had no sex for the last four years except with her own hand and her vibrators. And the only memory she had with her two boyfriends in college sucked. Now she knew they *really* sucked.

And though he'd given her orgasms the night of Hawk's wedding and again in the Camaro, he was now hitting a spot that...

"So fuckin' wet," he groaned against her breast.

That...

"Like I said, a fuckin' geyser."

His fingers dug hard into her ass cheeks as he held her right where he wanted her. Right where she wanted him to hold her.

Yessss, right there.

He lifted his head. "Gonna come?"

"Uh... huh."

"Like soon?"

"Uh... huh."

"Thank fuck," he grunted then shoved his face into her neck, sucking on her skin.

She closed her eyes, brushed her fingers over his short hair, trailed them down his neck and shoulders, then back up.

This felt so good, she could do this forever...

"Baby... *for fuck's sake.*"

"Okay," she whispered and let herself go, her core convulsing around him, the waves of orgasm washing up and over her.

He grunted loudly and pumped faster, no longer smooth, no longer gentle. His hips moved more wildly, more frantic. He slammed her hard, making her whole body quake with the impact.

And then with one last thrust, he grunted loudly in her ear and stilled while deep inside her.

Seconds, minutes ticked by and he didn't move. Finally, he unfroze himself and melted against her, his mouth to her ear. "Was gonna give you two, but you were holding out. Couldn't take anymore. I asked, you gave." He paused. "You can come on command?"

She shrugged. "I've been taking care of myself for the last few years. I'm pretty efficient when it comes to getting the job done."

He lifted his head and stared down at her. "What the fuck? Got so many questions after hearing that."

"Like?"

"Like... When's the last time you been with someone?" He added quickly, "Other than me."

"College."

His brows shot up. "That was over four years ago."

"Yeah," she whispered. Hell, it was actually more like five.

"Been with nobody for more than four fuckin' years?"

"I'm not going to ask you that same question. I already know the answer and we really don't need to be talking about our past sex life."

His fingers splayed along her cheeks as he held her in place, so she couldn't turn her head away. "Baby... You had no one since that first day I spotted you?"

"No."

"Why?"

She inhaled then released a long, slow breath. She wasn't sure if she should admit what she was about to. "Because I saw you."

CHAPTER NINE

Because I saw you.

B Those words kept spinning in Linc's head as he dismounted his sled and stared at the back door to church. His eye caught the sign that had hung above the reinforced steel door for decades. The club's motto.

Down & Dirty 'til Dead.

He had been almost twenty-four the first time he ever walked through that door to become a prospect...

Hell, he had no idea at the time how walking through that door would change his life.

Maybe some of the people in his past would think it didn't change him for the better. But they'd be wrong.

Dead fucking wrong.

The first thing he noticed after landing in Shadow Valley, was the DAMC. Their colors. Their Harleys. Their businesses. Their sense of community, inside and outside of their tight-knit club. He'd watch them roar by on their sleds in town, and they seemed to be badass and carefree. Though, now he knew the carefree part was a bunch of bullshit. The members had just as much responsibility as anyone outside of it. They answered to each other. They all had to work hard.

Shit wasn't easy.

Live free, die free.

Total fucking myth.

Down and dirty 'til dead? More realistic.

But even so, he loved this club, he belonged in this club. This club was his family. They took him in when he needed to land permanently somewhere, when he'd been drowning in a sea of shit and drifting aimlessly for far too long. This club had been his lifesaver.

Crow helped with that when Linc walked into In the Shadows Ink for the first time. After seeing the man's cut he wore proudly, Linc had asked him questions about the club. Surprisingly, the man had answered them. Then Linc went back for his second tattoo. Again for his third.

Before he knew it, he had a prospect cut on his back and was living in a small, shitty room above their clubhouse, helping Hawk tend bar and play bouncer by keeping the peace with any rowdy drunks.

He received no judgement. Only acceptance.

He owed each and every one of his brothers who voted to patch him in. To bring him into the fold on a permanent basis.

Up until now, he'd have to say that getting handed his full set of rockers was the best damn day of his life. But last night with Jayde in his arms... last night and this morning being inside of her. Knowing she was his now and would never be anybody else's?

Best. Damn. Day. Fucking. Ever.

But now as he headed toward the door, knowing who and what was waiting for him on the other side...

He knew this day might suck big time.

Especially when he noticed Axel's sled in the parking lot, too.

Reaching for the door and sucking in a breath to brace, he pulled it open.

As he let the door close behind him, he heard yelled across the common room, "Your asshole still puckered?"

Fuck. Yeah, this day was gonna suck.

Then as his eyes adjusted he saw Diesel bouncing Violet in his arms. Hawk wore some sort of fucking contraption that looked like a backpack worn backward, which kept Ashton facing his chest. And Z was keeping one eye on Zeke as he toddled around the floor, chasing a pool ball.

Jesus fuckin' Christ.

What the fuck happened to this MC?

He thought about the sonogram image he had tucked in his wallet and smiled.

Maybe they needed to change the sign over the door to say *Down & Dirty 'til Kids.*

J ayde stared at her now noticeably rounded belly in the mirror on the ceiling.

On the freaking ceiling.

Jewel said Jayde's cousin Jag had installed it when he lived in the apartment with Ivy. She never had Diesel take it down because... well... because there was nothing like Diesel's naked ass. And seeing the "Eighth Wonder of the World" while it was pumping and flexing was something Jewel admitted she didn't want to miss, even if that Wonder landed in her bed every night.

Which was why she most likely got pregnant when D told her they weren't having kids.

Right.

Now the big man, who Jewel called "the beast," didn't let his daughter out of his sight.

Luckily for them, the club's enforcer finally relented about moving into a cabin on Ace's farm to give his family some room. Since they left the apartment furnished, she and Linc had moved in the same day Diesel and Jewel moved out.

The only piece of furniture they moved in that was their very own was the crib Linc had bought on their first "date" three weeks ago. Now that was tucked into the corner of the small bedroom.

But this place was only temporary. At least until the baby was born. Because a one bedroom, one bath apartment over Shadow Valley Pawn wasn't going to cut it for very long.

Her gaze dropped from the large mirror when Linc walked back into the bedroom completely naked. He'd gone into the bathroom after they'd had sex for what seemed the hundredth time in this week alone.

Not that she was bitching, though her thighs and other places were a little sore. It was like he was trying to make up for lost time. She understood that completely.

She pushed herself up onto her elbows and studied his lean, muscular body that was full of tattoos above the waist. "Remind me to thank Slade." And Crow, too.

He stopped at the end of the bed, put his hands on his what she now called his *sexy flexy* hips and tilted his head. "For what?"

"When I first saw you, I thought you were hot. Now you've been working out with him, sparring, doing whatever you're doing, honing," she waved a hand up and down indicating his body, "all of that, you're not only hot but *freaking hot*."

He grinned and climbed onto the bed, stalking toward her on his hands and knees. "That get you wet?"

"What it got me was pregnant."

His grin twitched. "Yeah, it did."

She slapped his arm. "Oh, so *now* you're proud of that?"

"Couldn't have happened with a better woman."

Jayde pinned her lips together and blinked back the sting.

When she didn't answer, he continued, "Know this set-up ain't ideal. Gonna talk to Ace 'bout snagging a place on the farm when one opens up. Yeah?"

"Yeah," she mumbled, trying to get her shit together so she didn't start bawling. These guys could be complete misogynistic assholes that seemed to be uncaring and crude, but when they let something slip like he just did, it was both heart and panty melting.

Kiki warned her that the pregnancy hormones will turn her into an emotional mess at the drop of a hat. Which had to be the reason she burst into tears when Linc had insisted they put the sonogram images on the fridge and then he did just that. Jayde was pretty sure she scared the shit out of him by the sudden outburst of water works.

He might have even had second thoughts for a moment about moving in with her.

Fortunately, he hadn't gone running and screaming from the apartment. Instead, he was now settling under the sheets next to her with a sigh, pulling her tightly against his side. "Though, your brother's still talking 'bout building some sort of housing complex. Something gated, secure. Like a compound."

"Is that necessary? The Warriors are almost extinct." Or at least she thought they were. While no one had come out and said that for sure, there were rumors throughout the DAMC sisterhood that D's crew was whittling down their numbers.

"Almost, not quite yet. Talked 'bout that the other morning, too. Being nomads, D don't got any hard and fast numbers on how many are left."

"But didn't they lose their president recently?"

Linc's lips thinned out.

Of course. He wouldn't talk about the details. Club business wasn't women's business. But Jayde did know Brooke had something to do with that, or at least knew about what happened to the Warrior's last president. Even so, she never talked about it. Whether Dex had told her not to, or she just didn't want to bring it all back up, Jayde didn't know.

"Sure they got a new prez by now," Linc grumbled. "Now the DAMC's expanding with the next generation, Z wants to make sure everyone stays safe. D's on board with the complex, too." He shook his head and snorted. "That meeting was like a fuckin' nursery school. Hawk walking 'round with spit-up on his damn cut. I swear

D started lactating. Waiting on Z to start child proofing the common room at church since his kid likes to face plant on the regular. Our kid better not be so fuckin' klutzy."

Jayde pinned her lips together to keep from laughing because it didn't seem like Linc was joking.

She had only heard bits and pieces from that meeting since they hadn't had much chance to talk since then. Linc normally came home late from the bar and she was usually asleep when he did so. He'd wake her up just long enough for him to give her a couple of orgasms with those *sexy flexy* hips of his and then he'd roll off her and be snoring within minutes.

Tonight was the first night he'd come home at a decent hour since he convinced Jester to close down the bar. It was the first night that they'd actually had a chance to sit down and eat dinner together.

Jayde had to admit that it had been nice. And the look on Linc's face when he tasted her food and realized she could actually make something edible had been priceless.

He brushed the hair off her forehead and glanced down at her. "Cage been getting you back and forth to work okay? No problems?"

"No. But it's a piece of shit." She was driving an old Ford sedan that a customer had left at Shadow Valley Body Works because it would've cost too much to repair. So Crash took it, got it running, patched and primered some of the rust spots, and began to use it as a loaner. But, hell, it was nothing like her Camaro.

She missed that damn car.

"Gonna get you a good car for hauling the kid around. Like a minivan."

She jerked her head up. "What? No! No minivan!"

"Yeah. Somethin' safe, lots of room."

"No. Linc!"

He pinned his brows together. "Gettin' what you're gettin'. No lip."

"But—"

He grabbed her chin and forced her to look up at him. "Woman, gettin' a safe cage for you and the kid. Don't wanna hear no lip about it. Club's gonna pay for it and I'm gonna work extra hours to pay the club back. Got me?"

"A Volvo is safe," she suggested.

"Ain't gettin' no fuckin' Volvo. Christ, did you not hear me? Gotta work extra to pay it the fuck off. Want me working twenty-four seven?"

She groaned. "No. Maybe I can talk to my dad." Beg him to get her car back.

Linc jerked against her. "No. Ain't asking that man for nothing. I'm taking care of you now. My responsibility. Got me?"

"But I need to try to fix this with him, anyway, Linc."

"No, *he* needs to fix that shit. Not you. Don't need you begging for his forgiveness 'cause you're carrying *my* kid."

"I'm sure it was just a shock. He may have calmed down by now."

Linc cocked a brow at her. "Yeah? That what your mom said?"

Jayde opened her mouth, then snapped it shut. *Fuck.*

There were two reasons she didn't want to answer that. One, she hadn't told Linc she'd talked to her mom every day since that dinner. Two, because her mom did say her dad was still fuming. So badly, he still was barely talking to Axel. She was sure that made a pleasant time for them at the police department.

She felt for Bella, she really did. She had to straddle the line with her man being a cop and with her being pure DAMC.

And that's what Jayde may have to deal with in the future, as well. Her father and brother being cops while the future father of her child was DAMC.

Was it too much to ask for everyone to be fucking happy?

Of course it was.

Life could never be that simple. That would be way too easy.

"Gotta make something clear here and now, Jayde. Don't want you lying to me. Ever. Whatever you gotta tell me might piss me the fuck off, but I'll get over it. Plan on never lying to you, either. Got me? So gonna ask you, been talking to your mom?"

She tipped her eyes up to his face. "Yes."

His green eyes softened and the creases around them smoothed out. "Baby, she's your mom. You gotta talk to her. Ain't nothing wrong with that."

That's not what she expected him to say, so it surprised her. "I'm hoping she can help smooth things over with my father."

"Know you're hoping that, but not sure it'll happen. He still has a problem with Z. All these years he coulda got over it. He hasn't, even though he fuckin' knows Z was set-up for the shit that put him in prison. That man knows it and still..." Linc shook his head, clearly disgusted.

"It's not just about that, though, Linc. It's not. He worries. Z, even Axel, thinks he's scared. He doesn't want to deal with any more loss. He lost his father and his brother due to this club. He doesn't want to lose his son, too."

"By the way he acts, he already lost him. And he didn't need to. Fuckin' stubborn."

Jayde sighed. "Yes, he is. I doubt he's going to change."

"Gotta grandson he spends no fuckin' time with. Got a daughter-in-law who's the bomb. Z couldn't do any better than Sophie. Z has made this club successful, flush with cash. All legit, too. And that man still looks down on his own son. Doesn't matter what Z does, ain't good enough for him. And you know why?"

Jayde knew why, but Linc continued anyway.

"Cause he wears the DAMC colors on his fuckin' back."

"So do you."

"Right, so doubt he'll ever accept me or my kid, either. Maybe you just gotta face that. April visits Zeke on the sly. Maybe she'll have to do the same with our kid."

Our kid.

When Linc had stuck the sonogram photos to the fridge he said it was a reminder of what brought them together and where they were going. She couldn't believe how his view on becoming a father had changed. All it took was hearing that heartbeat and seeing his future son or daughter on a screen in a dark room.

"You didn't even want me to have this baby at first, now you're all in."

He curled up from his reclining position and dropped a hard kiss on her lips. "All in."

"I thought you said a child should know his or her grandparents."

"Yeah. But not if your dad's gonna be a total dick."

"Okay, then what about your parents? She, or he, will have them, right? Do they live close by?"

Jayde lifted her head when Linc went completely solid. She tipped her eyes up to the mirror and saw his expression had become completely closed off.

"Linc," she said softly. "I don't know anything about your family. Our baby's family." She placed a hand on her belly. A belly that housed a baby who'd be born in less than twenty-six weeks. "Don't you think I should?"

"This kid will have the club, that's plenty of family."

While that was true, that wasn't an answer Jayde wanted to hear. She lifted herself up onto her elbow and stared down into his face. He avoided meeting her gaze. "Linc."

He closed his eyes and his jaw got tight.

"They don't accept you?" she prodded. "Did they freeze you out like Dad did with Z? What?" He needed to tell her sometime. And she needed to know before the baby was born.

His moss green eyes finally flipped to hers. "We're making a family for this kid. He'll be fine."

"Linc..."

"Not talkin' about it now. Tired. Need sleep." He flipped over to his side, effectively cutting her off. Then he reached out and switched off the lamp on the nightstand. "Sleep," he ordered.

She stared at his back. As her eyes adjusted to the darkness, she could make out the rockers and insignia that Crow had inked permanently into Linc's skin. She reached out to trace them but curled her fingers into her palm instead and pulled her hand back. She rolled over, grabbed her phone from the charger and slipped out of bed.

"Where you going?" she heard him grumble, though he didn't turn to face her.

"The bathroom."

She rolled her eyes when she only got an answering grunt. Then she headed out into the hallway where the only bathroom in the apartment was. Turning on the light, she closed the door behind her. Of course she had to close the toilet seat and cover because that was left up, then she sat down and stared at her phone.

It was after eleven. She wondered if Z was still up. If not, he could answer her in the morning. She typed out a text: *What's the deal w/ Linc's fam? U know?*

She was surprised when her phone dinged almost immediately. She quickly muted it.

Yep, was the only answer her brother sent back.

She sighed. *R U going 2 tell me?*

Nope.

She scrubbed a hand down her face, then typed: *Don't U think I should know?*

Yep.

Jesus, her brother...

So? she prodded.

Not 4 me 2 say.

She let out a soft curse. *Got a baby on the way...*

No shit.

She gripped the phone harder because she had an urge to whip it across the tiny room and then stomp on it until it was in pieces.

Whatever, she answered, then hit the power button to turn off the screen.

CHAPTER TEN

This getting dropped off at the office every time the clunker wouldn't start, and then having to wait for him to pick her up in the afternoon was getting old. Especially when Linc was always late getting her there in the morning because he worked until the middle of the night and was just about impossible to get out of bed just a few short hours after he crashed. Then he always managed to be late picking her up before he had to work The Iron Horse.

The man needed a watch, that was for damn sure. Or a shock collar to get him moving on time.

Jayde dismounted the bike with a hand planted on Linc's broad shoulder to make sure she didn't fall on her ass. "I need a better car," she said for what seemed the thousandth time as he shut off the bike and yanked his bandana down from his lower face. "Every time that junker won't start, it's a struggle to wake you up and drag you out of bed, so I can get here. I need a decent car."

"Already got Rig towing it to the shop this morning."

"Okay, but here I am, late again. Kiki's going to have a fit. She's swamped with work, so it's not fair to her that I keep showing up late. And I need this job, Linc. Especially since I need a car, we have a baby on the way and I'm supposed to start classes again this fall."

Why did the thought of all of that make her overly anxious? She used to have a carefree life living with her parents. Now she was drowning in responsibility.

"She ain't gonna fire you."

"Maybe not, but I don't like putting the burden on her when I can't get here on time."

"Got it."

"Good." She hesitated. "So I need a car."

"Said that."

"Like soon."

"Crash is gonna fix the car today. Will get the prospects to drop it off here for you before you leave."

Jayde sighed. "But—" She shut up and tilted her head. "You hear that?"

A loud male voice. Yelling. Angry. Coming from inside. That wasn't good.

"Yeah," he grunted.

Her gaze slid through the parking lot. Two vehicles were there. Kiki's Vette and an old rusty Ford pickup.

"Know that vehicle?" Linc asked her as he swung a leg over his Harley.

"No."

"Stay here."

Oh sure. She was supposed to stay outside while he went inside to deal with whoever was yelling. Maybe Kiki needed her help.

She hesitated just long enough for Linc to yank the front door open and get a head start, then she followed.

As her eyes adjusted to the interior of the front office, she saw Kiki standing with her hands on her hips in her typical business attire, which was a business suit with a skirt that hugged her curvy hips and sky-high heels.

On the outside she seemed pretty calm and collected, but, even so, she was looking at Linc with relief.

A man, one Jayde recognized as a newer client, one who was

recently arrested for assault during a bar fight, stood screaming in Kiki's face.

Or at least until Linc collared him, yanked him away from Kiki and flung him to the ground. "He bothering you?" Linc asked in a low, dangerous voice. One that sent a shiver down Jayde's spine.

Kiki sighed and Jayde was surprised to see her hand shake as she raised it to smooth down her hair. "He's just a little upset."

"'Bout what?"

"His bill."

"Why's that?"

"Because he's blown through his retainer and I need more funds to continue with his defense." While Hawk's ol' lady's hand might be a little shaky, her voice sure wasn't.

Linc's green eyes landed on the guy who was grumbling out a string of curses and pushing himself up to his knees. He pointed a finger at the older man. "Stay right there 'til I figure out what the fuck's going on."

"Fuck you," the man with a receding hairline and a salt-and-pepper bushy beard said. "Paid the bitch to get me out of a jam. She ain't doin' shit and now she wants more money. Like I got it fuckin' growin' on a tree out at my place."

"Must be doin' something right since you're standing the fuck in this office and not in jail."

"Don't mean shit."

"Don't it?" Linc growled at him with an eyebrow cocked. Stepping in between him and Kiki, he kept an eye on the man who was still rising to his feet. Without looking at Kiki, he asked, "Want him removed?"

"I think that's for the best." Kiki glanced at her client. "Mr. Jones, you are now officially fired as my client. I will forward your paperwork to the attorney of your choosing, just have them contact me directly. I will also waive the balance that you owe me if you're smart and walk out of here like a civil human being. If Linc has to escort you out, then I'll make sure to sue you for my outstanding fees."

The man's face, which was red when she and Linc walked in, now got darker. "You can't fire me, bitch!"

Linc squared off with him. "The hell she can't. Now, gonna do what she asked and walk outta here with your balls intact? Or do I gotta *escort* you the fuck out?" When the man grumbled something unintelligible under his breath, Linc got a little louder. "Didn't hear a fuckin' answer. Got one more second to choose."

With more grumbling and a last glare at Kiki over Linc's shoulder, he turned around and headed toward the front door.

Jayde scrambled to give him space as he lumbered by her. She winced when the front door slammed and rattled the front picture window.

"Told you to wait outside."

Jayde's attention turned from where Jones disappeared back to Linc. "Kiki might've needed help."

"Yeah, that's exactly why I told you to wait the fuck outside."

"Linc..."

"Can't be giving me lip on this sort of shit. There was no way you were getting between Keeks and that asshole. Can't be putting yourself and our kid at risk like that. Got me? That asshole comes back, you call me, Hawk or D right away."

She thought he said the last part to Kiki, so she didn't answer, but then she realized Kiki had disappeared into her office.

Linc, with a serious look on his face went toe to toe with her, grabbed her chin and forced her to meet his gaze. "Got me?"

"Yes, I got you," she whispered.

He lowered his voice and another shiver skittered down her spine. "Care about you, baby. Don't want anything happening to you. Yeah?"

"Yeah," she breathed, unable to fight her smile at how protective he'd become.

He planted a kiss on her lips, then smacked her on the ass as he walked toward the front door. "Remember, he shows up again, call me, D or Hawk," he threw over his shoulder one more time.

Jayde didn't bother to answer because he was already gone and she needed to go check on Kiki. Maybe even call Hawk to let him know what happened, if Kiki hadn't done that already.

But speaking of Hawk, Jayde needed to have a little conversation with his brother after work.

"*Z*ak knows but won't tell me."

Diesel grunted.

Jayde pursed her lips in annoyance and studied the man sitting behind his desk at In the Shadows Security. There was no doubt that he wasn't happy that Jayde had invaded his domain. Well, she wasn't happy that she had to come to him, either. "Do you know?"

The big man grunted again.

She sighed loudly. "D, really. I'm having his kid. Don't you think I should know?"

Before she could get another grunt as an answer, the door opened and her cousin walked in with Violet in her arms.

Jewel froze at seeing Jayde, then unstuck herself. "Oops. Sorry. I didn't know anyone was in with D."

Jayde waved her hand around. "Doesn't matter." She stood, and Jewel came around the chair and gave her a one-arm hug.

"Congrats?" Jewel asked in Jayde's ear.

Jayde lifted one shoulder. "I know I had baby fever for a while with everyone getting pregnant and having babies, but having the urge and actually having one are two different things."

Jewel glanced down at Violet, who had a handful of her long, dark hair in her little fist. But her baby blue eyes were focused on her father as she let out a loud coo. "That's for damn sure."

"Thanks for giving up the apartment on short notice."

Jewel jerked a thumb toward Diesel who was now hen-pecking at a computer keyboard and staring intently at the screen like that would help plug his ears to the chatter of the two women. "Good excuse to finally get his ass moving and find us a place. You two should move out to the farm, too, once one of the other leases comes up on a cabin."

"Linc talked about that."

"That would be great. It would be nice to have a bunch of us with babies close by. If we can get Z and Sophie, too—"

"Fuck," D barked out.

"What's wrong?" Jayde asked him.

"Ain't a fuckin' coffee house. Go chatter elsewhere."

"But I came because of Linc..."

"What about him?" Jewel asked.

"I don't know anything about his family and he clams up every time I ask—"

With the knuckles of his fists planted on the desktop, D leaned forward and yelled, "Family's dead. Now get gone!"

Both Jayde's and Jewel's mouth dropped open and their eyes widened as they stared at each other for a moment before directing their attention back to D.

"What?" Jayde whispered.

"Dead. Get gone." His eyes landed on the baby. "Leave Vi."

"I need to nurse her, D," Jewel said with a look of exasperation.

"About Linc—" Jayde started, trying to get them back on topic.

"Then feed 'er an' leave 'er in here after," D ordered, ignoring Jayde.

"Then she'll shit in her diaper," Jewel snapped back. "You want to change it?"

D leaned back in his chair and stared silently at his ol' lady and daughter. The longer he stared at them the more his harsh expression changed. His eyes became warm, his face softened, and his frown flattened out as his dark eyes slid slowly over his woman.

Jayde blinked to make sure she was seeing what she was seeing. *Holy shit*, "the beast" had actual feelings?

Jewel was noticing his reaction, too. Her face changed, as well, a flush running up her chest into her cheeks and her eyes heated as she stared back at her ol' man.

Oh shit.

Time for Jayde to bail. Diesel liked to have sex against the wall. He was an expert at it and there was no way Jayde was sticking around to witness D nailing her cousin against an office wall.

That was a big, fat nope.

A loud clearing of a throat had all eyes sliding to the open doorway, where Ryder, one of D's "Shadows," was leaning in. "Sorry to interrupt, boss, but..."

D, his expression now shuttered, lifted his chin to him and Ryder stepped inside. He was carrying something in his hand.

Something Jayde recognized. And she wasn't the only one in the room who knew exactly what Ryder was carrying.

"Hey... this belong to either of you?" Ryder's eyes bounced from Jayde to Jewel. "Found it on the sink in the bathroom."

Someone left a pregnancy test stick on the sink at In the Shadows Security?

Uh oh.

"Does it have one or two lines?" Jayde asked, her heart racing as she watched Jewel's face turn a sickly shade of pale.

Ryder glanced down at it. "Got a plus sign."

Oh fuck.

Diesel shot to his feet, his chair flying back and crashing into the wall behind him. "Fuckin' woman!"

Jewel took a step backward, almost bumping into Jayde. "I—I... *fuck*... I was going to tell you tonight! I didn't want to tell you here. In front of anyone. And I wanted you sitting down this time."

"Not supposed to be a fuckin' *this time*!" Diesel roared, making Jayde wince.

Violet let out a little mew as Jewel clutched her to her chest tighter. "I know... I..."

He scrubbed an agitated hand over his short hair. "How the fuck did this happen?"

"Boss, think we had this discussion already," Ryder started with a snicker.

D pointed a beefy finger toward his open office door. "Get the fuck out. Now!"

Ryder's smirk widened, he plunked the positive test stick on D's desk, spun on his heels and left with a two-finger salute. "Yes, boss!"

Before D could continue his yelling, Ryder poked his head back into the office, "Congrats, by the way."

Then he disappeared, his loud laughter heard as he walked away.

D's dark brown eyes narrowed on his ol' lady. "What the fuck, Jewelee? Only been a few months since you had Vi."

"No one knows that better than me, and I'm still nursing her—"

"No shit," he barked.

"And I thought I couldn't get..." Her cousin's voice drifted away, and she grimaced as D's face turned a scary shade of red.

Oh shit.

At least it wasn't green or white, or whatever color it was when he passed out the first time he got the news Jewel was pregnant.

"I assume you put up a mirror on the ceiling at your new place?" Jayde asked, trying to keep her expression neutral.

"Get gone," Diesel growled. "Now."

Jayde lifted a palm. "But I need info—"

"Told you what I'm gonna tell you. Now get gone!" D roared, stomping around his desk and heading in their direction like a pissed off grizzly bear.

Oh shit.

"Fine," Jayde squeaked. She eyeballed Jewel who was frozen in her spot. "Text me if you need me."

Her cousin nodded, her gaze not leaving D as the man herded Jayde out of his office and slammed the door behind her. Hard enough that the walls rattled.

Well, that didn't go as planned. *Fuck.*

Now she'd have to do a little snooping on her own. She needed to know what she was dealing with when it came to Linc and his background.

She glanced down the corridor in the direction she hoped Ryder went.

From what she knew of D's guys, they were pretty cool. Deadly serious about their work. Pasts she probably didn't want to know anything about. But maybe one of them would be willing to help her out. They seemed to be protective of women in general.

She might be able to play that up and use that to her advantage.

She headed opposite of the direction the exit was and deeper into the warehouse where D and his men worked out of. Their "secret lair" which really wasn't so secret or a lair. It was a cavernous warehouse with offices in one part of it, secure storage in another and most of the remaining area was for keeping their equipment or whatever they needed for their assignments.

As she walked away from D's office, she knew he'd be pissed if he found out she was wandering around.

But hopefully Jewel was keeping him occupied.

No matter how pissed Diesel seemed, Jayde didn't worry about her cousin. Not for a moment. If anyone could tame that beast, it was the petite, outspoken Jewel. The two of them reminded her of a popular Disney story. One of Jayde's favorites, in fact.

As she got closer to an open doorway, she heard the clacking of computer keys. And soft singing.

She tilted her head and listened more carefully. Garth Brooks. *Friends in Low Places*. A low, deep voice that, if she hadn't already been pregnant by another man, might have made her ovaries explode.

Damn.

As she stepped into the doorway, she noticed Ryder was the one sitting behind the computer that had multiple large screens.

"That's you singing?"

His green eyes narrowed on her between the gap of two monitors. "Fuck. You caught me."

"Door was open."

He scrubbed a hand over his super short military-style haircut. "Yeah."

Ryder reminded her a lot of Linc. If Linc was a badass former Special Ops guy. Which he wasn't.

Or was he?

What did she really know about his past? She just knew he'd been part of the DAMC for the past four years or so.

The men had almost the same honey color hair, though Ryder's was a little lighter and a little bit shorter, but not by much. And their eyes were similar. That rich green. "You sounded good." Ryder was definitely handsome in a badass motherfucker type of way.

She had to remind herself that Linc's baby was in her belly right now.

"Right," he grunted.

She stepped into the room, which was pretty large and held several computers and a hell of a lot of monitors.

Badass central.

"D raging?" he asked.

"Not sure. I was kicked out of his office."

"He'll get over it. They're probably fuckin' about now. They're always in there fuckin'."

If they were, Jayde hoped Violet was taking a nap in the playpen that was tucked into the corner of D's office. "Hence the pregnancies."

He chuckled. "Yeah. Man's smart as fuck, but apparently not smart enough to take precautions."

"Speaking of... I have a question for you," she started.

He groaned.

She moved around the desk he was working at so she could see him better. Possibly gauge his facial expressions. Though the few times she'd been around any of D's guys, they were pros at hiding shit. "Do you know anything about Linc and his family?"

His face closed up like a Venus Flytrap with its prey. Which was about what she expected.

"You talking about Andrew Lincoln?"

Andrew Lincoln?

Holy shit, she didn't even know the real name of her own baby's father? After all these years?

"Um, yeah. You know another Linc?"

Ryder pursed his lips, then grunted, "Nope."

"Then, yes, him." Andrew. Andrew Lincoln. *Shit.*

"After that shit with Slade, D had us run backgrounds on all the newer members and prospects."

Interesting. "And what do you know?"

His dark eyes flicked toward the open doorway, then back to Jayde. "Why you need to know what I know?"

She pressed her blouse to her slightly rounded gut. "I'm not getting fat. I'm pregnant."

"Jesus, what the fuck's in the water at church?" He shook his dark blond head, then pinned his breath-taking green eyes back on Jayde. "So, what does that have to do with Linc's family?"

"Pregnant with Linc's kid," she clarified.

Ryder cocked a brow. "He know?"

"Definitely."

"Good thing I ain't taggin' any of the DAMC women, because, *fuck*, I'm not ready to be a father any time soon." He frowned. "Or ever."

"Apparently we're fertile."

"Right. So you're having Linc's kid, but he ain't talking about his family." He tilted his head. "Or his past, right? That why you're in here bugging me?"

She flipped her index finger at him. "Bingo."

"D wouldn't say shit?"

"Bingo again."

Ryder sighed and crossed his beefy arms over his especially beefy chest. And though his chest and those arms looked awesome in that tight black T-shirt he was wearing, she was pretty sure they'd look even more awesome without it.

"This gonna get me canned?"

Ryder smirked at her when she lifted her eyes after roaming his chest. "No."

He cocked a brow. "You sure?"

"No."

J ayde leaned back in her comfy leather office chair and rubbed a
   hand over her eyes. This pregnancy thing was exhausting. It
   was like the kid was sucking the energy right out of her. She
swore she was growing a vampire inside her and not a baby.

Maybe she should just take a cat nap on her desk while she
waited for Linc, if only her full bladder would allow it.

He was supposed to come pick her up and take her to the ultrasound. She would have met him there if it wasn't for that piece of
shit loaner car not starting this morning. *Again.* Instead he dropped
her off at work on his sled and said he'd pick her up at four.

It was now five minutes after four and their appointment was at
four thirty. Which meant they might be late if he didn't show
up soon.

But her eyes were drooping, and the office was quiet since Kiki
wasn't around. When the club's attorney was there, the office was
like a whirlwind. She was so busy and had the energy of three people.
It tired Jayde just to watch her. But Ashton had been colicky, and
Hawk was at his wit's end with worry, so Kiki went home early to
deal with both her men.

So the only thing keeping her company at that point was the
large jug of water she had been chugging to prepare for the ultrasound. And to keep her mind off of how badly she needed to pee and
how that was only going to get worse—especially riding on his bike
—before it got better, she leaned her head back, closed her eyes and
for the thousandth time thought about what Ryder had revealed to
her over a month ago.

She wanted to talk to Linc about it. But she also wanted him to
come to her. She didn't want to confront him with what she
found out.

So she waited. And waited. She figured he'd get really pissed at
her for digging into his past, so she preferred he told her himself.
Though he told her to never lie to him, she wasn't *technically* lying.
She was only omitting what she'd done. Besides, if they were going to
make a family, this was important information she needed to know.

Whether he agreed or not.

Which he probably wouldn't.

But he'd have to get over it.

She sighed. However, now she knew and was tired of sitting on that information. And it was almost impossible to not let that slip.

That day, Ryder had told her to close the door, so they'd have a warning if D came in and caught them. Which sounded much naughtier than it should.

The corners of her lips curved for a second at the thought of being naughty with one of D's Shadows. She sighed and pushed the fantasy that would never happen out of her head. No one warned her that being pregnant would put her sexual libido into overdrive.

She frowned when she thought about what Ryder showed her.

He had brought up several newspaper articles on the computer. More than several. So many that it made her head spin. And then spin some more when he began to point them out and give her the gist of each of them so she wouldn't have to read them all.

He also pulled up pictures. Some were from Linc in high school. No tattoos. Smiling. Carefree. An athletic, muscular body even back then. Pictures included him in a football uniform sporting his school's logo. Pictures of him wearing a singlet and posing in a wrestler's stance. More of him holding trophies by himself. Standing in a group of other young wrestlers. Pictures of him on a mat actually wrestling at matches. Prom pictures. Old Facebook photos of him standing next to a new Mustang convertible. Pictures of him standing with an arm hanging around a pretty girl's neck with a sly, relaxed smile on his face.

Pictures of him camping with what seemed to be his family. His parents and a younger sister that had the same maple syrup hair color as Linc. And most likely the same moss green eyes.

But it wasn't all of those pictures that twisted her gut and made her heart seize. Or the articles claiming Andrew Lincoln, a 4.0 student, was a champion wrestler and was being scouted by some great colleges.

No.

Though, she had to admit, all of that had surprised her. But what broke her heart was the news articles, the police reports, the coroner's reports that she had no idea how Ryder could have access to. Nor did she ask...

Her eyes skimmed these things Ryder brought up on the oversized monitors as he talked. And talked. Giving her the lowdown on Linc's past and family.

Giving her the reason Linc most likely ended up somewhere other than where his family was from. Why he ended up one night at In the Shadows Ink. Why Crow had talked him into prospecting for the DAMC.

Because the "boy" had been lost. At eighteen, he had nothing left. He walked away from his future because he could no longer see it clearly.

He had not only lost his sight of that future, he thought he lost everything.

And it took him years to find something similar to replace that loss.

At almost twenty-four, the club had taken him in and then let him become "Abe" while he was a prospect. Then around twenty-five he became "Linc" as a fully-patched member.

Slowly, he rediscovered himself. Discovered his future. Found his place in life again.

Until Jayde had dropped the bomb on him about being pregnant.

No wonder he'd suggested what he had.

But after hearing all those words Ryder spilled, Jayde didn't think Linc would ever be Andrew Lincoln again.

Which was most likely why she'd thought Linc's first name was Lincoln, not his last.

She wondered how much Zak knew about Linc. She figured he knew some, but maybe not all.

That didn't matter. What mattered was that Linc and her needed to talk about it. They were now a couple, weren't they? They lived together for over a month now, they were having a kid together. She assumed Linc would claim her at the table eventually. Make her his official ol' lady.

They should probably even get married, but she wanted to hold off on that until her parents could be there. So they could take part. Have her father give her away.

Didn't every little girl dream of her daddy giving her away?

She huffed out a breath.

Hell might freeze over before then.

Maybe more realistically, they needed to wait until they loved each other. Because at this point, there was an attraction—always had been—but Jayde knew that was about all there was. She hoped love would eventually come, as well, for the sake of their child.

Her hand slid over her belly. She was four and a half months along now. They'd find out the baby's gender today and she wanted to get a better idea of her due date. She hoped today's ultrasound would give her that.

She also wanted Linc to be standing by her side.

Still, he needed to show up soon, so they didn't miss their appointment.

She opened her eyes and grabbed her phone. She hated to text him since he was on his bike and couldn't answer if he was on his way. She certainly didn't want to distract him.

But she was getting concerned when she looked at the time. It was now a quarter after four and time was going to be tight.

She released a sigh of relief when the front door to the office opened.

Finally.

CHAPTER ELEVEN

Fuck. Fuck. Fuck.

He was fucking late. He always seemed to be late no matter how hard he tried not to be. Why the fuck couldn't he not be late?

Jayde was going to be fucking pissed if she missed her ultrasound appointment. Which would mean he probably would have to listen to a whole bunch of bitching. Luckily, while on the bike, he'd get a reprieve. At least temporarily.

He pulled his sled into the parking lot of Kiki's law firm and was surprised to not see the woman's Vette there. He parked in front of the door, shut off the engine and kicked down the stand with his boot heel.

He stared at the fancy freshly repainted sign on the side of the building as he yanked down the bandana covering his lower face. *K. Clarke-Dougherty, Attorney-at-Law.*

Maybe eventually it would need to be repainted again to say *Clarke-Dougherty & Lincoln, Attorneys-at-Law.*

His chest puffed out a little at that thought. No matter what happened, no matter how hard things got financially, he would make sure Jayde continued to work toward her law degree. This accident of theirs was not going to ruin her life or her dreams.

He'd figure it out. Right now he just needed to get his woman to her appointment. The kid in her belly was part of their future. A future that was going to change drastically in a few short months.

He dismounted and tried the door.

Locked.

He furrowed his brows and pounded on the door with the heel of his fist. "Jayde, let's go. Gonna be late."

He received no answer. After pounding once more, he placed his ear to the door to see if he could hear her moving around inside, gathering all the shit women insisted they needed to carry with them.

Nope. Nothing.

Fuck.

His eyes scanned the empty parking lot. Maybe Kiki took Jayde to the doctor since his ass was running late.

That would make a hell of a lot of sense.

But for fuck's sake, he was looking forward to this appointment. He'd not only hear that heartbeat again, but they'd find out whether they were having a boy or a girl.

He wanted to be a part of that. He *needed* to be a part of that. He had to show her that he was all in this one hundred fucking percent, so he wanted to be by her side at every appointment.

He dug his phone out of his pocket. No texts or calls from Jayde. Not one. Not one telling him she got a ride. Not one bitching about him being late.

Nothing.

His heart thumped in his chest as he pulled up Hawk's number and hit the green icon on his cell.

"Yeah," came the gruff answer.

"Kiki take Jayde to her appointment? Got fuckin' tied up and they ain't here. Office is locked up. Not a damn vehicle in the lot."

Hawk's gravelly voice sounded suspiciously cautious when he asked, "What time is her appointment?"

His heart thumped a little faster. "Four thirty."

Silence. Way too long of a hesitation for Linc's liking.

The hair on the back of Linc's neck stood up when Hawk answered, "Kiki's here with me."

Linc heard Hawk's woman in the background. "What's going on?"

"Linc's at the office to pick up Jayde for the ultrasound an' she ain't there."

After another long hesitation which didn't make him any calmer, he heard Kiki suggest, "Maybe one of the other girls gave her a ride."

"Hear that?" Hawk said into the phone.

"Yeah. Heard it. Keeks know the address of her doctor?"

Hawk blew out a loud breath. "Yeah. She should. Same one she goes to." His voice became a little more distant. "Babe, need the address for your doc. An' then call 'em an' make sure Jayde arrived for her appointment. Got me?"

"Let me call them first," Linc heard Kiki tell Hawk.

"No," Linc said into the phone. "Wanna start heading over there. Don't wanna miss it."

"Don't fuckin' blame you. Every time you hear that heartbeat, shit gets real. Then when you find out whether you're havin' a son or baby girl... *Fuck*..."

"Right," Linc breathed. "So, the address..."

"Brother, she's already on the phone with 'em."

Linc could now hear his own heartbeat pounding in his ears as he waited to find out if Jayde had caught a ride with someone else. Probably to spite him since he'd been late.

Hawk ground out a curse before saying directly into Linc's ear, "No, ain't there. You go inside?"

"No. Door's locked." Linc could only hope that Jayde rescheduled the appointment and got a ride back to their apartment instead.

"She try textin' or callin' you?"

"No."

Hawk's voice was tinged with impatience when he asked, "You try textin' or callin' her?"

"Will do that next."

"Gonna head over there with the key. Be there in ten. Try callin' her soon as we hang up. Yeah?"

"Yeah."

"Call me if you find her. Otherwise, stay put 'til I get there."

"Yeah."

"Gettin' Keeks to call all the women. See who she's with. Have her call Bella to ask Axel to contact her parents since Z can't call 'em. Maybe she just went home."

There was no way she went home to her parents. No matter how pissed she had become. "Hawk, she had an appointment. An important one."

"Yeah. But she's a woman. Sometimes shit don't make sense with 'em."

"Hawk!" Linc heard Kiki yell.

"What?" Hawk grunted.

"Good Lord, that was rude."

"Babe, call the women. Start a fuckin' phone tree. Somethin'." He sighed into the phone. "Hangin' up. Sit tight. Got me?"

"Yeah."

Their call disconnected and Linc stared at his phone. He scrolled to his recent calls, found Jayde's number and put the phone back to his ear.

When he got her voicemail, he left a message, then texted her.

And for the next ten or so minutes he kept doing it over and over, hoping she'd pick up during one of those calls or at least text him back.

She didn't.

He should've felt better when he heard Hawk's sled roaring into the parking lot.

He didn't.

And what they found out between Kiki's phone tree and what was inside the office made everything so much fucking worse.

A xel screamed at Diesel as he strode across the room, "Get your men on this now! Right now!" He looked at Hawk. "Get the Dark Knights on this, too. Right away. I don't care what they fucking have to do to find her and get her back. Just fucking have them do it."

D's brown eyes narrowed on the off-duty cop as he approached.

The women, none of whom had seen Jayde or even talked to her, had been instructed to head out to Ace's farm where Slade, Ace, and the prospects were on guard to keep them and the kids safe.

Until they knew what the fuck happened to Jayde, everything was on lock-down. Everyone was on high-alert.

"Sure she's not just pissed at somethin' Linc did? Women get fuckin' crazy when their hormones are fucked up," Jag suggested.

He should know, Ivy was almost ready to pop out their first kid.

Jag continued, "Sometimes they're like Sybil."

"Who?" Dex asked, confusion pinning his eyebrows low.

"That chick with a million an' one personalities," Jag explained. "Jayde could just be fuckin' with Linc since he was late. Just a fuckin' minute late an' they go off the fuckin' deep end."

A few grumbles of agreement filled the room.

"An', for fuck's sake, let one rip in bed durin' the fuckin' night an' you might wake up with a fuckin' knife in your back," Dex added.

Axel threw his hands up. "Really? My fucking sister's missing." His eyes slid to Linc. "My *pregnant* sister."

"We all fuckin' know what the fuckin' issue is, pig," Diesel barked. "Already dealin' with it, so keep your fuckin' panties on."

Axel's jaw got tight and he turned his attention to Z. "What do you have so far?"

"Not much," the DAMC president told his brother. "Linc went to pick 'er up for her ultrasound an' she was gone. Office was locked. He an' Hawk went in an' found the office chair turned over, the papers from the desk all over the floor. Both her an' Keeks' computers were missin'. Kiki had a small safe that's gone, too."

"Fuck," Axel said, scraping one hand over his head while the other was planted on his hip. He blew out a breath. "Dad's got the PD on it. Going to get a detective over to the office to check for prints and any clues. Who's over there waiting to meet them?"

D grunted, "Got Steel waitin'."

"Probably fucking up the scene," Axel grumbled.

"Does a better job than you fuck faces!" D exploded. "Couldn't even figure out that Z had been set-up, you fuckin' stupid motherfuckers!"

Axel's head jerked back at D's outburst. Jayde's brother's face got dark and his blue eyes narrowed, but he was smart enough not to go toe to toe with D. Especially since the club's enforcer could knock Axel out with one punch. He had not only done so in the past, but might not hesitate to do it again in the future.

Crow came up behind Linc and gave his shoulder a firm squeeze. "You holdin' up?"

Linc shook his head and stared at his boots. "All my fault. Fucked up. Being fuckin' late. Again. Mighta stopped whatever happened if I'd been there on time."

"Don't know that."

"Right," Linc grunted.

"Don't even know what the fuck happened."

Truth was, everyone knew something bad happened. If it wasn't for the safe and the computers missing, her disappearance could've been chocked up to her being angry with him. But there was no way Jayde was staging her own struggle and then hauling a safe, which weighed too much for her, out the door. Even her pregnancy hormones wouldn't make her that whacked to stage something like that.

"Was supposed to be finding out today what she's having, not looking for my woman, wondering if she's okay. Hoping—" He stopped since his voice was getting thick and was about to crack.

He needed to keep his shit together. For Jayde. For his unborn son or daughter.

"Hear ya, brother. We'll find 'er," Crow said softly. "D's crew's good at findin' people. Know that the Knights are already on the lookout an' have their ears to the ground. An' we're all headin' out shortly."

Linc let his gaze slice through the room. His gaze bounced off all his brothers who'd gathered to help find his woman. "We assume it was the Warriors but could be random."

"Could be," Crow agreed. "Don't matter who it is. Gonna pay either way."

Linc nodded.

"Nobody fucks with DAMC property," Dawg growled, joining them. "Nobody fucks with our women. I'm headin' out now. Gonna do some scoutin'. You comin'?" he asked Crow. "D wants us out in pairs."

Crow nodded. "Yeah." He slapped Linc on the back. "Gonna find 'er, brother. Promise."

"Yeah," Linc muttered. He only hoped when they did, she was safe and unharmed.

One thing that bothered him was the last time the Angels had a run-in with the Warriors, when Pierce had sicced them on Dex and Brooke back in Harrisburg, something had been said by the Warrior's president—may that fucker burn in hell. But what he said now stuck in Linc's mind... They were planning on taking over Shadow Valley, taking out all of the DAMC kids and planting their own babies in the DAMC women's bellies.

While it was only a crazy-assed threat that could never happen, that didn't mean some of those unstable fuckers wouldn't try.

They'd do anything to stick it to the Angels. Now the Dark Knights, too. Even so, they kept fucking with the wrong MCs. The Knights weren't going to curl up and disappear, either. They now had a hard-on for the Warriors as much as the DAMC, and almost as much as D's Shadows.

"Gotta roll, brother," came from his right. *Zak*. Worry lines creased his president's face. "You're with Hawk, got me? I'll deal with Axel's ass."

"Got you." Linc lifted his head and met Z's gaze. "Have any idea where to even fuckin' look?"

Something crossed Z's face that didn't give Linc confidence. "Truth? No. Don't even know it's the Warriors. Can only assume it's their ass-fuckery."

"Yeah."

"Just gotta hit every empty, deserted building an' house within a twenty-mile radius. D's crew's spreading out beyond that area. Puttin' the word out. Cops are lookin', too. Axel said the PD put out a state-wide BOLO."

BOLO. *Be on the lookout.*

His guts twisted. "Whoever it is... if they touched her... Took her..." His nostrils flared, and his fingers clenched into fists. "Wanna find them before the pigs."

"That's a fuckin' given," Z agreed. "But there's more 5-0 than us. Especially with Mitch on the warpath. Those pigs are gonna search harder for a cop's daughter an' sister than the average folk. Count on that. Either way, don't matter who finds her, just gotta get her back safe."

Wasn't that the fucking truth.

Hawk approached, his face hard, unreadable as he stared at Linc. "Ready, brother?"

Linc nodded and his hand automatically went to touch the gun he'd shoved into the back waistband of his jeans, which was concealed by his cut. "Yeah."

Both peeled off from Z and headed toward the back door.

"Gonna keep your shit together?" Hawk asked him.

"Yep."

Hawk grunted. "Been in your fuckin' shoes, brother. Know how this shit will eat at you, fuck with your head. Just don't do anythin' stupid, got me?"

"Yeah."

"If my ol' lady had been pregnant when those motherfuckers took her..." he shook his mohawked and tattooed head. "*Fuck.* That's all I'm sayin'."

And that was all Hawk needed to say. The shit that went down with Kiki and Jazz had been a fucking nightmare. Because of the abuse Jazz went through, she never came back to Shadow Valley, even after she was physically healed. Not even for a visit.

No one blamed her. She needed time to get over it. Unfortunately, Shadow Valley and the DAMC were nothing but a reminder. Just like his hometown was one of his reminders.

So, if Jayde even went through half of what Jazz had at the Warrior's hands...

"D get her phone pinged?" Linc asked as they strode quickly to their sleds.

"Yeah. Steel found it on the floor at the office under some papers that were tossed."

Fuck. They'd missed that when they searched the office earlier.

Hawk jerked his chin toward their sleds. "Let's ride."

CHAPTER TWELVE

"Soon as she wakes up, we'll get her to open the safe."

Jayde kept her eyes squeezed shut at those words. There was no way in hell she wanted those assholes to know she had come around. She struggled to keep from wincing at the pain from her splitting headache.

"Bet there's a lot of cash in there."

Stupid idiots. There was *no* cash in the safe. Kiki had no reason to keep money at the office. She only kept important paperwork in it because the safe was fireproof and had come with the property. Otherwise, she probably wouldn't have one at all.

And if she had kept cash in it, the safe would most likely had been bolted down to the damn floor.

What a bunch of bumbling idiots.

"Know someone with a torch."

"Easier for her just to give us the combination."

"Yeah, if she was a-fucking-wake. But she ain't. Shouldn't have hit her so hard, dickhead."

"She fucking kneed me in the nuts. It was instinct."

Jayde heard a snort.

Jesus. Her head was pounding, and she might even be bleeding where the guy hit her. She was afraid to lift her hand to check.

She had no idea who these fools were. She had no idea where she was.

What she did know was they were a bunch of turds that were going to regret the actions they took.

After they had busted into the office, she had hoped Linc would show up while the three man-boys were still there. Unfortunately, he didn't.

They ended up pushing her around until she got mad enough to knee the one asshole in his family jewels. And once she made the short, skinny one drop to his knees with a strategic strike, the guy dragged her down to the floor with him and everything went black shortly after that.

One thing was for sure, these assholes were not Warriors. They were just a bunch of two-bit thieves. Stupid ones at that.

However, now they weren't only thieves, they were officially kidnappers and would also be charged with aggravated assault. Or simple assault. Whatever. She should have paid more attention when her father was talking about work while at the dinner table.

Still, she wondered how they even knew about the safe in Kiki's back office. She couldn't figure out if one of them had been a client since Kiki did criminal defense.

"Better be a lot of dough in there to make this all worthwhile."

"Pop said as much as that lawyer charged 'im, the bitch should be rollin' in it. And if the bitch's rollin' in it, then that safe should be stuffed full of green."

Jayde pinned her lips together to prevent informing them about how stupid they really were.

Because doing that wouldn't help her one bit.

No, as long as they thought she was passed out, they'd leave her alone. Hopefully.

But the one mentioned their pop. She had a feeling their father was the one Linc kicked out of the office, the one who had given Kiki shit.

"Maybe we can shoot it open," one of the geniuses suggested.

While Jayde listened to the three stooges argue about the easiest way to open the safe, she mentally did a full body check. She wasn't tied up, which was dumb on their part, but good for her.

Besides the punch to the head or whatever the asshole did to knock her out, she didn't think they hurt her anywhere else. They weren't professionals and most likely had no idea who she was. To them, she was just someone who'd been between them and the safe they thought was going to be a windfall. When it wasn't.

They were going to be extremely disappointed.

So, she needed to delay. She hoped Linc had finally showed up at the office, figured out what happened, and got everyone out looking for her.

Her father was already not thrilled about her working for a criminal defense attorney who also was the club's attorney. But now?

This might just be another good reason, in his eyes, to get on his soapbox about her staying away from the DAMC. And Linc. As well as finding another job.

It would be another "I told you so," like he'd thrown in Zak's face in the past.

She might as well kiss her father accepting Linc or his child goodbye. All because of these amateur *Ocean's Eleven* wannabes.

"Gotta get her awake," she heard close by.

She opened her eyes just a slit, just enough to try to get her bearings. She was in what looked like a barn. A barn that wasn't used to house animals, though. Maybe it was an equipment shed. Or equipment barn.

Or whatever. Holy hell, whatever it was she didn't want to be there.

But she had a feeling no one would find her there. Not her father, not Axel, not the Shadow Valley PD.

Not Linc. Not D's Shadows. Nobody.

Her pulse sped up and her breathing shallowed.

She had no idea where her phone was, either. She tried to swallow the lump that was creeping up her throat, but it was impossible. She needed to keep her cool. Needed to keep the panic at the possibility of no one finding her at bay.

She needed to keep thinking clearly so she could figure out a way to get out of that situation. She needed to save herself. Get her and her baby out of there safely.

These weren't Warriors. They weren't after revenge. They most likely didn't want to harm her or kill her. These guys weren't hardened criminals, they were just complete fools who were trying to do a thing and she just happened to be at the wrong place at the wrong time.

She was not the target. They didn't want her, they wanted cash.

To replace their missing teeth. Or to get a better functioning brain. Or whatever the idiots wanted.

She had both DAMC and cop blood running through her veins. And that thought bolstered her. She could do this. She could get herself out of this mess.

It was also important to get her hands on one of their phones. Even if only long enough to dial 9-1-1.

Peeking through her lashes, she noticed the three masterminds standing around the safe, staring at it with hands on their hips. Maybe they were trying to open it with their genius brain waves.

She shifted her hand enough to slide it over the rise of her belly. When the taller one looked in her direction, she squeezed her eyes shut again.

Shit.

"Think she moved."

"What?"

"Think she fucking moved. Think she's awake. Her hand wasn't there before."

"Where?"

"There. On her gut."

Stupid move, Jayde!

Multiple footsteps headed in her direction.

A sneaker poked at her leg. "Know you're awake."

"Shake her."

"You shake her."

"Damn pussies," the closest man-boy said.

Then one of them was yanking on her hair, actually trying to pull her to her feet using a handful of it.

She gasped at the sharp sting to her scalp.

"Told you she was a-fucking-wake!"

"Drag her over to the safe."

"Drag her by her fucking hair since she was tryin' to fake us out."

Jayde opened her eyes and stared at the guy who had her hair in his fist. Maybe she could talk her way out of this. Reason with them. "I don't know the combination."

He gave her hair a hard yank. "Bullshit, bitch."

"Even if I did, there's no cash in it."

"Bullshit," the short one she had kneed in the balls echoed.

"Just open it and we'll let you go."

Sure. Sounded believable.

She lifted a hand to the tender spot on her head and winced again. "I have no reason to know the combination since there's nothing of importance in the safe. It was left behind by the former property owner."

"She's lying."

"I'm not. Best thing you could do is let me go," she said as calmly as possible. "You have no idea who I am and you don't want to."

"You ain't nobody."

She kept from rolling her eyes. "Where do you want me to start?"

"Don't give a flying fuck who you are. Just open the safe."

"I would if I could because I'd love to see your faces once it's open and you realize you fucked up."

The tall one, Stooge One, released her hair and stepped back.

She rubbed her scalp. "Can I get up?"

"No, don't you move," what looked like the youngest one, Stooge Three, said. They all looked alike. Definitely brothers, but different ages.

The middle one, Stooge Two, chimed in. "She's gotta be lying. Pop said—"

"Your pop is wrong," Jayde told him, sitting up and wrapping her arms around her middle.

"Watch your mouth," Stooge One yelled.

She needed to try and reason with them. "Look, you don't want me. You want money, right?"

All three of them just stared at her like three baby owls on a low-hanging branch, none of them blinking.

"I can make a call and—"

"No!"

"Yes, I can call someone to give you money in exchange for letting me go."

All three of them continued to gawk at her like brainless idiots.

"It's simple." She held her palm out. "Just give me one of your phones, I'll make a call and have someone bring a bunch of cash here when they pick me up. How much do you need?"

"A million dollars," Stooge One answered.

Jayde almost choked. "You... You expected a million dollars in the safe?"

"No, but now you're offering, that's what we want."

"Yeah," Stooge Three agreed.

Was she imagining all of this? She had to be. Maybe she had become light-headed, passed out at the office and banged her head. Because this couldn't be happening. But if it really was... "Okay, I'll have someone bring out a million dollars."

Their eyes went wide. "Really?"

Jayde lifted a shoulder. "Sure. The club's got plenty of money."

The three exchanged glances before dropping their gaze back to her.

"What club?" Stooge One asked, his dark eyes narrowed.

"Dirty Angels MC," she answered.

Silence. More looks exchanged. This time with worry.

"You're not DAMC," Stooge One told her.

She shrugged again. "Okay, don't believe me, then. Your loss." She flipped a hand in the direction of the safe. "That belongs to the DAMC, too."

All six eyeballs landed on the safe. Two of the idiots went pale. But the third one, Stooge One, the one that looked and acted like the leader didn't pale at all, instead he directed his narrowed eyes back on Jayde.

His chin lifted ever so slightly and he looked smug. "Our uncle is a Warrior."

Oh shit.

"He might be interested in a DAMC bitch. Know you're lying about the DAMC having a million dollars to save your ass, thinkin' we're stupid. But I'm sure the Warriors might pay something for you."

"My dad and brother are cops!" she exclaimed quickly.

The oldest one grinned. "That might be even better. Sweeten the pot some." He glanced at his younger brothers. "Watch her close. Gonna go call Uncle Scratch."

Uncle Scratch?

As soon as Stooge One walked outside, she turned her attention to the other two. "Look, you don't want to do this. You don't want to make enemies of not only the DAMC but the SVPD."

The short one shrugged and spat tobacco juice at her feet, splashing her. She fought her gag reflex.

"Need cash. Warriors will give us cash for you."

"The DAMC has more," she insisted.

"How you know?"

"I said I'm DAMC..." She let the insult of calling him "asshole" drift off. "My brother's the club president."

"Even better."

She opened her mouth, but snapped it shut when Stooge One walked back into the shed/barn/whatever the fuck it was.

"Scratch wants her for sure."

"How much he giving us?"

"Thousand bucks."

Jayde pursed her lips. Now she was only worth a thousand? Did she get discounted? Yellow tagged? "I thought you wanted a million."

The tall guy shrugged. "Nobody's got a million and he'll be here in twenty minutes. Don't have to worry about your fuckin' kin taking us out, either. A grand will get us cold beer, fat steaks and fuel up the truck."

It'll also get them time in prison for kidnapping and human trafficking, but she wasn't going to point that out.

"Now's a good time to let me leave and point me to the nearest road." Her gaze landed on the cell phone the oldest one still had in his hand. She needed to get her hands on that. She cried out sharply and let out a sharp hiss. "Shit! My legs are cramping. Help me up." She lifted her hands toward Stooge One. "Please, just let me work out these cramps." As the three man-boys closed in on her, she pushed to her knees and held out her hand again to their leader. "Please, help me up. Just for a few minutes before your Uncle Itch gets here. *Ooow*."

As Stooge One grabbed her arm, she jerked back sharply, pulling him off balance. She grabbed at his old flip phone but missed. She watched it tumble to the ground in slow motion.

No!

She dove for it but so did all three of the country bumpkins. Somehow she got her fingers around the phone first as they grappled with her to take it from her hand.

She flipped it open and...

She cursed in frustration when the phone was plucked from her fingers by Stooge One. "Nice try. Now we have to tie you up."

Oh shit.

"Get some rope," Stooge One ordered.

"From where?"

"Anywhere! Check the truck," Stooge One shouted.

Stooge Two or Three, whichever, ran out of the building while Stooge One stood over her, frowning. "That was just stupid," he told her.

She agreed.

Within a few seconds, the man-boy who had run out to the truck came back with a handful of twine. If they managed to tie her up, she was screwed. She'd never escape and she'd end up in the hands of the Warriors, which was far worse than these bumbling bumpkins.

If these idiots knew who the DAMC were and robbed Kiki's office, it meant they were local. Which also meant she probably was being held close to town. If the Warriors got their hands on her, she could end up anywhere. Including underground in a dirt grave in some random field.

Their uncle was less than twenty minutes out, that meant she had to form a better plan. And she needed to do it quickly. However, since she bungled the plan to get the phone, they were going to be more vigilant.

"Hurry, tie her up," Stooge One ordered.

"It's tangled up."

"Untangle it."

"What the hell does it look like I'm doing?"

"Being slow, that's what."

Jayde kept a careful eye on Stooge Two as he struggled to untangle the mess in his hands. Stooge One and Three also watched him impatiently.

Which meant they weren't watching her.

She bound to her feet and surged forward in the direction of the exit. Stooge Three stepped in her way to block her, and using all her strength, she shoved him hard and scooted to the right, barely avoiding his grasp.

Then Stooge One tackled her from behind. When she fell forward and hit the floor all the air rushed from her lungs.

She gasped, trying to catch her breath, but she couldn't. Even though he was tall and skinny, he weighed more than her and used that weight to pin her down to the ground. She did her best to flip around in an attempt to knock him off her, but it was useless. Trying another tactic, she used her hands and feet to pull herself along the floor toward the door. But Stooge One was screaming at her to stop and ordering the other two to help grab her and hold her down.

There was no way she'd be able to escape all three of them pinning her in place.

She eyeballed the door of the shed. It wasn't that far. Only about ten feet. She needed to fight her way to it. She needed to get the hell out of this shed before Scratch and maybe even more Warriors arrived.

She gritted her teeth and surged upward, trying to knock the oldest one off of her. But just when she was making headway, one of his brothers sat on her legs and the other snagged one of her wrists.

Fuck!

She wanted to cry with the futility of it all. But she couldn't. She needed to stay strong, needed to stay mad and not give up.

She couldn't give up. She had an unborn child to protect.

"You're all dead. Dead! They'll kill your uncle when they rescue me and then come back and kill you all. All of you. Your pop won't have a single son left to carry on his name. Dead! All of you!"

Stooge One laughed. "No one even knows where you are, stupid bitch. Just us and Scratch. No one's going to find you or *rescue* you. And for a thousand bucks, I couldn't give a shit what my uncle and his MC does to you."

She tried to keep her voice level. "You will."

"Doubt that. Tie her up," he ordered again, sitting on the small of her back, grabbing both wrists and yanking her arms behind her. "I'll hold her, you tie."

"No!" Jayde screamed, struggling even harder.

By some miracle she was able to pry one hand loose. She swung her arm until her hand struck one of them. She curved her fingers and clawed down his cheek, ripping it open, drawing blood and screams as he released her.

She swung again and made impact with another one. She closed her fist and began to beat him wherever she could make contact. Finally, figuring out where his most sensitive parts were, she used all her strength to punch him in the groin as hard as she could.

More screams. A little more freedom.

She twisted her body as hard as she could. It was now or never. Stooge One, who was scrambling to get a hold of her arms again, was thrown off balance and he fell to the side. She pulled in her knee then kicked him as hard as she could in the gut. He collapsed onto his side with a howl.

She was free! She twisted again, rising to her hands and knees. All she had to do was crawl out of there before they could grab her again.

She could do this. This was life or death.

Panting and trying to gather strength, she pulled herself toward the door. She could see the daylight coming from underneath it. She could smell freedom.

Then an impact hit her so hard she lost her breath once again. Then another. And another.

Someone was kicking her. No, not someone...

All of them.

She dropped to the ground, curled into herself, wrapping her arms around her middle, trying to protect her stomach.

"*No! No. Please...* No! Don't! Not my stomach. Don't... Please!" But no matter how much she begged, no matter how much she fought to protect her belly, the kicks kept coming.

She could no longer hear anything except for her own endless pleas, she could no longer see anything through her tears. Her body throbbed in every spot they made contact. Dizziness swirled through her and she pulled her knees tighter into her chest.

She was going to be all right. They were going to be all right.

It wasn't going to end like this. It couldn't.

But all Jayde could do at that point was try to continue to breathe. Grit her teeth against the sharp pains that shot through her. Her chest. Her belly. Her back. Her ribs.

Then cramps twisted her insides. Warm fluid slipped from between her legs. But she couldn't move.

She wasn't sure when the kicking ended because she floated in and out of consciousness. It could've been seconds, minutes or hours later when she heard a gruff voice say from a distance, "Why she got blood down there? You rape 'er?"

Helplessness and hopelessness swept through her, bogged her down as her sobbing became unstoppable.

Scratch had arrived.

CHAPTER THIRTEEN

More men. A flash of a furious face. Strange noises. Grunts. Thumps. Scrambling.

Bits and pieces washed in and out of her consciousness.

Then voices. Deep. Pissed. Worried.

That couldn't be good.

Multiple conversations at once spun in her brain.

"Boss... yeah... found her..."

"Z... got her."

"Needs medical. Have him meet her at the hospital."

She tried hard to lift her heavy eyelids. She cracked one open long enough to see Mercy kneeling by her side, pressing his fingers to her wrist. His face, normally severe, was savage.

"B—baby," she managed to get out. Though, even that was a struggle due to the pain in her jaw and ribs.

His eyes met hers and he only grunted. He lifted his scarred face, jerked his chin and said, "Steel assigned transport. Get on it quick."

"PD en route."

"Right. Leave those three motherfuckers for them. Take the Warrior."

"Copy that."

Someone scooped her up and stood. She cried out because everything hurt so badly. She was broken.

Completely shattered.

No doctor could fix that.

"Sorry, baby. Know it hurts. Just hang on. Gotta carry you."

She pressed her face into whoever's chest she was being held
against and began to cry all over again.

Her eyes popped open at the sound of a hair-raising howl down
the hallway. Whoever it was sounded like their world just
came to an end.

She knew the feeling.

But Jayde also knew whoever it was, it wasn't Linc.

Definitely not Linc.

No, because Linc's furious voice could be heard outside her
hospital room door. "Going the fuck in there!"

And her father's equally furious answer, "You're not going
anywhere near her! This whole thing is over."

"Bull-fuckin'-shit! We live together."

"Not anymore."

"Honey," she heard her mother say. "Let him go in for a few
minutes. Let him see she's okay."

"She's not okay." Her father's voice broke, which tore at Jayde's
heart even more. Her father was so strong and stubborn, and for him
to break... "And now there's no reason for him to even be near her."

"Dad, let him in." *Axel.*

"Have you lost your fucking mind, son? Ever since—"

"Don't," Axel's response was as sharp as a shard of glass before
turning thick with pure grief. "Just don't. Not here. Not now. Let
him in."

There was a shuffling outside the door, then it opened. That's
when she realized her eyes were squeezed shut and one of her hands
shakily covered her mouth.

A squeal of a chair filled the room as someone pulled it close to the bed. Then that someone was holding her hand. A forehead was pressed to her shoulder and warm breath swept over her.

Someone.

Linc.

He was simply there. Quiet. Unmoving.

A presence she should find soothing, but she wasn't sure if she did.

The room swirled with sorrow, regret and anger. So thick, she could taste it on her tongue, feel it against her skin. It crept along her spine, burrowed into her center.

She lifted her bruised hand with the needle stuck in it and lightly touched his hair. When he lifted his head, she whispered, "I'm sorry."

His green eyes were haunted, his expression tortured. Seeing that made her insides hurt more than they already did. The ache in her heart became even more unbearable.

He hadn't wanted the baby at first. But he now mourned.

His eyes, his face, the curve of his normally broad shoulders showed her that this had wrecked him.

She wanted to cry for him, but she couldn't. She was empty and no longer had any tears left to shed.

"Got nothing to be sorry about, baby. Did nothing wrong. It was me. I fucked up. I'm the one who's sorry. You don't... You don't know how sorry I am."

He was feeling guilty about being late. While she could understand that, he needed to know it wasn't his fault, either.

It was just bad timing. Bad luck. Bad... *everything.*

Her voice quivered uncontrollably when she told him, "I did my best to protect him..."

Their unborn son.

During one of her conscious moments she had demanded to know and they reluctantly told her.

He squeezed her hand tighter. "Know it, Jayde. Don't doubt that for a fuckin' second. Can see what they did to you. Know you did everything you could do to protect yourself. Protect him. I fucked up."

"No—"

"Shoulda been there on time. Shoulda been there to save you. My job to protect you. Didn't... Couldn't do any of those things. Failed you. Failed our son. Failed your family..." He choked on his next words. "Failed *our* family."

His words of defeat ripped what pieces remained of her broken heart right out of her chest.

"Always late. No excuse. Just a fuck up."

"Linc..."

He pressed his forehead to their clasped hands. "So fuckin' sorry, Jayde. Don't know how to fix this, make it better. Don't know what to fuckin' do."

She didn't know what to tell him, what to say... because she didn't have any answers. Even if she did, it wouldn't change a thing.

She tried to swallow, but her mouth tasted like it was full of sawdust. "How... How did they find me?"

He shot a glance toward the door before lowering his voice. "Turns out D's crew's been trailing that Warrior since the fucker lives local. Tailing him to find more of the nomads. Luckily, one of them jumped on his tail when they heard you were missing. Fucker led them right to that barn. To you." He blew out a breath. "Thank fuck for that, but... I couldn't even fuckin' be the one to find you."

Linc's explanation circled her brain. How ironic that a Warrior helped save her in an around-about way. "You're being too hard on yourself."

He ignored that, and his gaze roamed over her, though he couldn't see much of her. He couldn't see most of the bruises or the binding that wrapped her ribs since she had a sheet pulled up to her armpits. But it was hard to miss when his gaze paused on her belly, on the slight curve that remained as a reminder of what was lost.

A place in her that had been full of life, now...

Was not.

His voice was thin when he asked, "How you feeling?"

"Tired." That was a simple answer to a complex question since she was feeling a lot of things. Too many to want to recognize or admit to.

"Pain?"

She didn't know where to begin to explain to him the pain she was experiencing. But he meant physical pain, so she simply shook her head. "Not much anymore. Strong pain meds…"

He glanced up at the morphine drip. "Yeah." Clearing his throat, he shifted in his seat and whispered, "Jayde…"

She lifted her free hand and shook her head slightly, closing her eyes to the undeniable agony in his.

They've never declared love for each other, so now they could go their separate ways. She could continue on her original path; he could continue on his.

Nothing tied them together any more.

He had no reason to stick around. The only reason he did so no longer existed.

"Jayde…"

"No, don't. You don't need to step up anymore when I know you didn't want to in the first place. You're free, Linc. We made a mistake. The mistake was erased. And now we're back to where we were before that night."

W*e made a mistake. The mistake was erased. The mistake was erased.*

The mistake was erased?

Jesus fucking Christ.

She didn't want to be with him now that the baby was gone?

His fingers twitched in hers. "No… Jayde… that's not—"

The door opening behind him made Linc sit up and shut up. He groaned under his breath when he saw it was not only Jayde's mother, April, coming in, but Mitch.

Fuck me.

Jayde twisted her fingers out of his grip and put her hands back on the bed. She avoided Linc's eyes, instead keeping them on her father.

April rushed over. "I couldn't stand outside in the hallway anymore, Linc. Sorry, honey." She moved next to his chair, touching the top of his head lightly, then touching Jayde's cheek with a gentle, but sad smile on her face.

April was a good woman even though she was married to a stubborn asshole. She raised three good kids. She loved and accepted them no matter what, even if she had to keep one of them at a distance to keep the peace with her husband.

Linc stood up and offered his seat to her, which she accepted with a quick squeeze to his hand.

Jayde's gaze dropped from her father's hard expression to her mother. April's eyes were shadowed and red-rimmed, her face pale. Her light brown hair was pulled back into a messy ponytail.

"Mom, who was out there yelling?"

April turned her troubled brown eyes toward the closed door and frowned. "Diesel's on a tear right now, sweetie."

"He okay?"

April shook her head, worrying her bottom lip. "I don't know. He left."

Shit.

"Probably will do something stupid and get his ass in a bind," Mitch grumbled.

Linc stiffened and turned on him. "Why do you even fuckin' care? You don't give a shit about anybody in the club."

Mitch's nostrils flared, and his jaw tightened.

"Not even your own fuckin' son. Not even your grandson."

Mitch held his gaze and didn't even have the decency to look away or be embarrassed about how he treated his own son.

"Linc..." Jayde whispered.

"Woulda been the same with me and my son." He heard a strangled noise behind him but ignored it. "You forget the DAMC's in your blood, too. You act all high and fuckin' mighty. You—"

Mitch pointed a finger at the bed. "See what happens being a part of the DAMC? Need I remind you who else suffered besides Jayde because of being a part of your club?"

No, Linc didn't need a reminder. He knew.

Mitch continued, "My daughter's laying in a hospital bed right now, injured, in pain, suffering with a major loss because of that club."

"And you're probably happy 'bout that last part."

April sucked in a sharp breath.

"No, Dad, it had nothing to do with—" Jayde started, but Mitch cut her off.

"She dodged a bullet," Mitch stated, staring straight at Linc.

She dodged a bullet?

A chill seeped into Linc's bones, froze every sinew of muscle.

Was he saying she was lucky she lost his child?

He couldn't move. Couldn't think. He wasn't sure if he could take a breath. Or whether his heart even continued to beat.

Mitch's shoulders were squared off, stiff, pulled back and he was ready for Linc to come at him.

The man expected a reaction from Linc. He wanted to make a point. Mitch wanted to prove to himself, or Jayde, or even April, that Linc wasn't worthy, that he was just a biker with base instincts. That he couldn't think with his head, just with his fists.

Linc's gaze slid to Jayde as she lay in that hospital bed. Her face ghost white, her eyes wide and red, a single tear slipping down her cheek, the sheets held in a death grip within her fingers.

But it was her mouth that caught his attention. It didn't quiver. Not once. She kept her lips pressed together firmly. The woman had just been through hell and back and she was doing her best not to shatter.

Because of that, she didn't need the father of her lost baby fighting with her own father.

Not now. Not ever.

With a nod, he pushed past Mitch and walked out of the room. Walked straight out of the hospital.

And he didn't stop walking.

CHAPTER FOURTEEN

L inc stared at the fridge, the black and white images stuck with magnets to the door. His nostrils flared, and he swallowed hard since his throat felt like it was closing up. He wasn't going to lose it. He wasn't going to break down.

He needed to remain strong while he removed the reminders of what could have been.

He braced himself as he slowly, and with care, removed the images one by one, unsure of what to do with them. He glanced at the garbage can nearby, but he couldn't make himself do it. He couldn't just throw them away like they had meant nothing.

Because they had. They meant more to him than what Jayde probably realized.

He should've told her just how much.

But he didn't. Again, he fucked up.

He slipped them into an opening he'd sliced into the lining of his cut, then moved to the bedroom. His eyes were immediately drawn to the crib in the corner. The one he insisted on putting together instead of the delivery guys. He had wanted his own hands to assemble the place his son would sleep. It had taken him longer than expected but it had been worth it.

Especially when Jayde had sat on the bed with the instructions in her hand, laughing at his lack of skill with a screwdriver. But he showed her. He finished it and it hadn't fallen apart. Then he had tackled her on the bed, making her laughter turn into a squeal, then moans and sighs.

He closed his eyes and his fingers curled into fists.

Why? Why did he have to lose everything he loved?

Every. Fucking. Thing.

What did he do to deserve any of it?

He wished he knew because he'd fix it if he could. He'd do anything to make it right.

With his jaw set, he lifted his foot and slammed his heavy boot into the crib. He didn't stop until there was nothing left to splinter.

He couldn't do it. He couldn't stay at the apartment over the pawn shop anymore. He couldn't stay there without Jayde.

He couldn't lay in that big bed staring up at the mirror while she remained in a hospital bed.

In the past, he'd always slept by himself. Then only with Jayde once they moved into their place together.

Now he didn't want to sleep alone.

But he had no choice.

She wasn't coming back to their place.

She wasn't coming back to him.

And he couldn't bear to see her side of the bed empty. He couldn't stand to hear the quiet. He couldn't bear the loneliness that had seeped into his bones.

After he had taken the pieces of the destroyed crib out to the dumpster, he'd gone on a long ride, in an attempt to clear his head. To try to figure out what to do next.

But he just couldn't.

Instead, he headed south into West Virginia and didn't stop until he hit the cemetery.

He'd stayed there all night.

After propping the sonogram images against the base of the headstones, he'd laid in the grass in the center of the three graves. He positioned himself directly over his father's final resting place. He stretched out his arms until he could touch the edge of his sister's to the left and his mother's to the right.

Everyone he'd ever loved had left him. And he could have prevented it.

Him.

He could've done something about it. But he hadn't. He fucked up.

He should've been on time to pick up Jayde. But he wasn't. He fucked up.

He was a hollow shell with nothing left on the inside. Completely empty and lost.

Jayde was right. He hadn't wanted that baby.

Until he did.

And now he didn't even have that.

As the morning sun rose above the horizon and a fog covered the ground, he picked himself up off the grass, his body leaving a silhouette behind like a ghost in the dew. When he mounted his sled again, he wasn't sure where to go.

West Virginia was no longer home.

And he wasn't sure if he wanted to return to Shadow Valley.

Though he loved his brothers, right now he couldn't muster up anything.

Dead.

He was dead inside.

Seeing Jayde in that hospital bed, her face swollen and bruised, her arms discolored, too. Bandages and IVs. Flecks of dried blood in her hair and on her skin that someone hadn't taken the time to wash away. The stitches over her left eye. Her swollen lip.

The slight mound of her belly that no longer held his son.

He didn't realize just how much he wanted him until after he was gone. And now Linc knew there hadn't been anything he wanted more.

Except for Jayde.

His second chance for a family had splintered into a million tiny fragments. And he had no idea how to put those pieces back together again.

None.

Grief and hopelessness ate at his insides as he mounted his sled, hit the starter and headed back north with his past at his back and his unknown future before him.

Hours later, he pulled up to In the Shadows Ink and through the large picture window that made up the shop's storefront, he saw Crow hunched over his drawing table, most likely designing a custom piece for a customer.

Crow glanced up, spotted him through the window and moved away from the table toward the front door. Within seconds it opened, and Crow filled the doorway.

"Brother," he greeted. His voice was soft, heavy with sorrow.

Linc wanted to go in, but he was having a tough time getting off his sled. He wasn't sure if what he was about to do was a good idea.

But then, did it matter?

"Brother," Crow murmured again, his brows furrowed low. "Linc..."

Linc nodded and when he could finally move, swung his leg over his bike, and headed inside with Crow.

Crow squeezed his arm, his almost-black eyes troubled, and asked, "How's Jayde?"

"I don't know."

"Brother... why're you here instead of the hospital?"

Linc shook his head. "Not wanted there."

Crow's dark eyes searched Linc's face, then he just nodded. "Whataya need?"

"Some ink."

Crow nodded again. "Lemme get set up. Know what you want?"

"Yeah."

"I need to draw somethin' up?"

"No."

Crow gave him a single solemn nod once more. "Got it. Gimme a few."

For the next ten minutes, Linc stood in the center of the tattoo shop, almost as if in a daze, as he watched Crow prepare the tattoo chair by wrapping it with plastic. Squeeze black ink into tiny cups, test his tattoo machine with the foot pedal.

When he was ready, Crow called out, "Where at?" and jerked his chin in an indication for Linc to come over.

Where at? The only place he could imagine. "Over my heart."

Crows lips thinned, and his nostrils flared slightly, before saying, "Don't got a lot of space there."

"Gonna be small."

Crow cleared his throat roughly, then murmured, "Right." His expression remained shuttered as he watched Linc shed his cut and then peel off his tee.

After Linc settled onto the chair, Crow reclined it. Moving the light stand closer, he wiped down Linc's skin over where his heart used to be, then waited.

After a few silent minutes, Crow finally murmured, "Gotta say it sometime. Gotta get it out."

Linc's eyes flicked to him then back up to the ceiling. "Yeah..." He let the name swirl around in his mind, before releasing it out into the world. "Jaymes." Then he spelled it out slowly, taking his time to carefully say each letter, to make sure he didn't break while he did.

Crow said nothing. Only put his head down and began to work.

When he was done, Crow pushed back, wiped the tattoo down, then covered it with A&D Ointment. He lifted his chin, silently telling Linc to go look at it in the full-length mirror on the wall.

Linc sucked in a deep breath, once again tried to swallow down the lump in his throat that never seemed to disappear, and headed over to the mirror.

It took a few moments until he was able to let his gaze drop to the fresh tattoo. To those raised, black scrolled letters over his heart.

They were small, because Crow was right, he didn't have much skin that wasn't previously inked. But he could see them and that was all that mattered.

"Don't let him stop you from getting what you want," Crow said softly.

Linc knew who Crow was talking about without him saying it.

"You two have wanted each other for years now. Understood why you didn't go after what you wanted. That shit's tough. See Axel an' Bella dealin' with it, makes it hard on their relationship. Z's now accepted the fact that shit ain't ever gonna change. Hopin' one day it does but can't say it ever will. Doesn't mean she ain't meant for you. You'd know it if she was. You'd feel that shit right under the spot where I just gave you that ink."

He stared at Crow in the mirror since the older man was standing directly behind him. "Know what that feels like?"

Crow shook his head, his long jet-black braid sliding across his back. "Can't say I do. Somethin' 'bout us brothers, though. When it's right, we know it. We fight for it, no matter what. We move those barriers, even if they seem to be an endless range of unscalable mountains."

He turned to watch Crow move away to pick up Linc's T-shirt and bring it back over to him. Linc gripped it tightly as the ink slinger continued.

"We've all watched you an' Jayde circle each other. All knew it was comin'. Just didn't know when. Jaymes wasn't a fuckin' mistake. He was a way to finally bring you two together. Gotta look at him as if he was your guide. Now it's in your hands what you fuckin' do with what he gave you, brother. Gonna waste that opportunity or use it?"

Linc opened his mouth to admit he had no idea what he was going to do, but Crow's next words made him rethink that.

"If you're feelin' what you're feelin', how do you think Jayde's feelin'? She dealt with a lot of shit. Gonna deal with more 'cause of Mitch. An' you just walked away. Brother, think," he tapped his finger against his temple. "You want her. She needs to know it. Wanna help her through this, then you fuckin' *help... her... through...*

this. Her loss. Your loss. Fuck Mitch. Show her what she means to you. Share your strength with her. She's gonna need it."

"I don't know, brother."

"You know. Just wait 'til the cloud clears, you'll see the light. Promise you that."

Linc hoped Crow was right. But then Crow was right all those years ago when Linc stumbled across his tattoo shop and the long-time DAMC member said that his club would be perfect for Linc.

Crow's wisdom was legendary in the club. He was rarely wrong. It was also rare when he didn't know the right things to say.

The man had a gift.

Linc tugged his shirt over his head.

"Know the drill. Keep it clean. Clean T-shirt, ointment. Got me?"

"Yeah." Linc moved over to where his cut was hanging on the back of a chair. He stared at the rockers and insignia for a moment.

He ran his fingers over the top patch. *Dirty Angels*. Then the bottom. *Shadow Valley*.

"Put on your colors, take a breath, then go take care of your woman."

With a slight nod, Linc shrugged his cut over his shoulders and walked out the door.

CHAPTER FIFTEEN

"What the fuck you doin' here?"

Linc released the tap once the pint glass was full and ignored Hawk. He moved down to the end of the bar and slid the beer in front of the waiting customer.

A large hand gripped the back of his neck and he was forcefully whipped around to face the man. Linc raised his fists to defend himself, but Hawk released him and shook his head. Linc realized it was disappointment more than anger that filled the larger man's eyes.

"Kitchen. Now."

Without waiting for Linc, Hawk lumbered toward the double-swinging doors as he grumbled curses under his breath. Linc did a chin lift to Jester, who stood with his mouth hanging open after watching that exchange, for him to take over serving the customers.

He reluctantly followed Hawk into the busy kitchen. The club's VP ignored the hustling staff and swung on Linc, pointing a finger back toward The Iron Horse. "What the fuck you doin'?"

Linc shrugged. "Working."

"Got fuckin' eyes in my head. Wanna know why."

Linc stared at his boots for a long moment, gathered his shit, then lifted his gaze until it met Hawk's. "'Cause I don't know what else to fuckin' do."

Hawk's head jerked back. "Whataya mean?"

"Don't know what else to do. I got nothing else."

Hawk's chest visibly expanded before blowing out a loud, long breath. "Nothin' wrong with takin' some time to figure shit out. Got the bar covered. Didn't expect you to work it right now."

"Need to work."

Hawk stared at him for a moment and then nodded. "Yeah," he grunted. "Heard you stayed upstairs last night."

"Yeah."

Hawk pursed his lips as he studied Linc for a minute. "Jayde's home."

The way she had looked in the hospital and with everything that happened to her, he expected her to remain there longer. He had also figured that Mitch had taken up sentry outside her room and would have blocked him from seeing her, anyway. "Already?"

"Yeah. Keeks an' Bella went over to help April get 'er set up, get 'er comfortable." He paused, then with a rough voice said, "When Keeks got... When Keeks..." Hawk cleared his throat, shook his head, then tried again. "When the Warriors fucked with her, her asshole ex came to the hospital an' tried to take 'er home. There was no fuckin' way I was lettin' him take care of my woman." Hawk gave him a hard look. "Got me?"

Yeah, he got what Hawk was saying.

"So give it a couple days if you gotta. Let her parents coddle her. But then go get your fuckin' woman. Got me?" When Linc didn't answer him, Hawk continued, "Brother, she's your woman, right?"

"Fuck yeah," he released on a breath.

Hawk nodded at his answer. "Then you know what to do."

Yeah, he had to convince Jayde that she was his woman. Baby or no baby.

Mitch or no Mitch.

Shit.

Crow was right. Hawk was right. But he needed to talk to Z first.

Linc needed to make sure he wasn't pissing Zak off by taking what was his.

Which was his president's sister.

———

Linc's heart thumped heavily in his chest as he dropped his fist and waited for someone to open the front door. A bead of sweat popped out on his forehead and he quickly wiped it away. He didn't think it was from the hot summer weather. No, it might be from the same fucking reason his asshole was a bit puckered right now.

He cursed under his breath when he heard heavy footsteps coming his way.

The door opened, and Mitch Jamison's initial surprise quickly turned into a scowl. "Not sure why you're here. But whatever the reason is, just get it out of your head, turn around and leave. You're trespassing."

Linc set his jaw. "Not leaving. Never should've left her hospital room."

"You did the right thing leaving. Now do it again."

Linc shook his head. "It was my job to protect her. My job to protect my kid. I fuckin' failed. I fucked up."

"No chance of that happening again since you're going to turn around and leave. Do the right thing, boy. Do it for her. She doesn't need to be a part of that shit and you know it. Look where it landed her."

Look where it landed her.

"I wanna see her." Linc said, his heart thumping like a bass drum in his chest after hearing Jayde's father's words.

"No chance of that happening, either."

Linc tried to look past his body, which was blocking the doorway. Linc was slightly bigger than him, so he could take the man if he needed to. But he'd rather do this another way. For Jayde's sake. "Wanna see her. I'm taking her home."

"She is home."

No. It used to be but wasn't any longer. Her home was with him. What he said out loud was, "No reason for her to be living with her parents. She's a grown woman."

He should know better than to try to rationalize with the man. He would never give in. Never be convinced. Linc might as well bang his head against the brick face of the Jamisons' house.

Mitch took a step forward but Linc held his ground. Pulling his shoulders back, he waited. There was no way he was leaving without Jayde. Even if he had to do it bleeding.

But the cop only closed the door behind him, stepped out onto the porch, and said, "I know your background, Lincoln. I did a check. I know who you are. I know where you came from and I know where you were headed. I know what happened. Even so, I'm not sure how you got off the right tracks onto the wrong ones. Not sure why you gave up everything to have nothing. But it makes me even more disappointed in you that you had the world by the balls and you just let them go. You gave up. My daughter needs better than a quitter."

Wrong tracks. Nothing. You gave up. A quitter.

No matter how much he wanted to argue those facts, he couldn't. "Your daughter deserves the best."

"And that's not you."

Mitch was right, but Linc wasn't going to admit it to Jayde's father. Instead, he would continue the good fight. "And that's where you're wrong."

Mitch shook his head and made a noise. "What in the hell do you have to offer her? You wanted a piece of ass, you got it. You got jammed up. You're now unjammed."

Linc jerked his head back and went solid, growling, "Ain't a piece of ass."

"You're right, she's not. I just made my point, Andrew. She's not a piece of ass. She has a good future, but that future will be tarnished if she's with you. She has goals that will remain unfulfilled if she ends ups with a damn biker like you. There's a reason I kept my kids away from that club. Do you think I like that my grandson will be raised in that hell? No. I fucking hate it. I have no say in that matter, but with Jayde I do. She's the only one left that I can save from it all. Zak's in so deep he'll never see the light. Axel's now skating on the edge. I'm not going to let my only daughter fall into that quagmire. And by being with you, that's what will happen. She'll never be safe. She deserves better than that. She deserves better than you." He tilted his head and studied Linc. "You could've made something of yourself. You had a future. You threw it all away. If you feel anything for my daughter, you won't want her to do the same."

After listening to the man's little "lecture," Linc had one of this own. "If you know everything about me than you know I've lost everyone I've ever loved. But I'm not willing to lose Jayde. So no matter what you say, no matter what you do, I'm not walking away from her. You can't keep her locked up in your house forever. Telling you right now, I'm gonna fight for her. And I don't want this to fuck up her relationship with you. I want you in her life, even if you refuse to ever let me in your house or eat at your table. I'm okay with that. Want you and April in our kids' lives. Because we *will* have kids and family's important. So fuckin' important. She loves you. Loves her mother. Hoping she loves me. If not, I'm hoping she'll give me a shot and come to love me. Wanna do right by her, but not by walking away. That's not doing her right. She isn't a little girl anymore. She's a woman, and you need to see her as such. You need to respect her decisions, even if they aren't the ones that you think she should make. You fucked up with Z. You could fix things with your son if you wanted to. Figuring it kills you to not spend time with your only grandchild. Just gotta fix it. Gotta accept your kids are gonna make mistakes, make their own decisions, even ones you don't like. Doesn't mean you should shut them out." He dropped his head and shook it. "Only wished my family was still around. I miss them every day. They would've loved her." He raised his gaze to meet Mitch's, whose expression was guarded. "You don't know what a gift you have. One you're wasting. One day you're gonna realize you missed out on seeing your grandchildren get grown. And you're gonna kick yourself when you do. Don't make the same mistake you made with Z with Jayde." Linc sucked in a breath. "You said you know me. But do you really? You only read shit on paper. Probably read reports, newspaper articles." He pounded on his own chest with his palm. "But you don't know me in here."

Linc took one breath, then two, then offered his hand to Jayde's father. To the man who was a cop, the one who could very well have him arrested for trespassing. One who could make his life a living hell.

Mitch's gaze dropped and he stared at it in surprise.

"Gonna give you some respect and expect the same from you. Just asking you to give me a chance. Let me prove myself. After that, if you don't like me, not gonna hold it against you. Do it for you, for April, for Jayde and your future grandchildren."

At that, Linc shut up, but kept his hand up and out between them. He wasn't dropping it until the man punched him, walked away or accepted it.

Linc kept his face blank but cleared the thickness from his throat when Mitch reached out and grasped his outstretched hand. With a firm shake, Linc dug deep and said, "Nice to meet you, sir. Andrew Lincoln. And I'd be forever grateful if you'd allow me to date your daughter."

"**K**now you deserve someone better. Someone who can take care of you, protect you. For fuck's sake, that ain't me. That's been proven."

The pain medication she was on must be screwing with her head. Because that sounded like Linc and there was no way in hell her father would allow Linc in his house.

"Should let you go. Let you find someone who'll do better, be better than me."

And he definitely wouldn't allow a member of the DAMC into her bedroom. Unless hell had frozen over?

Jayde opened her eyes and turned her head. She wasn't dreaming. Linc was sitting on her bed in her bedroom in her parents' home.

She glanced toward the window. Nope. It was still a sunny summer day outside. Nothing appeared frozen.

"Then why are you here?" she asked softly.

"'Cause I'm a selfish fuck and you belong to me, Jayde. No one else. Can't let anyone claim you but me. Might not be the best for you, but every day gonna try to do my fuckin' best. Promise you that. Some days I'm gonna fuck up, but I'll try twice as hard the next day."

She didn't know what to say to that because she still wasn't sure what was happening wasn't a hallucination. "How did you get in? The window?"

"The front door."

Huh. Her father usually insisted on keeping the front door locked. "My mom let you in?"

"No, your pop."

Yep, she was hallucinating. She closed her eyes and settled back into the pillow. She apparently needed more sleep and less drugs.

Then fingers, warm and long, intertwined with hers. "Baby." The low murmur certainly sounded real. The fingers connected with hers seemed real, too.

But there was no way her father let Linc into his house. "I'm just imagining you, Linc. You're not really here."

More fingers, this time sweeping over her cheek, then brushing the hair away from her face. A light kiss to her forehead. Warm breath gliding over her skin.

Those pills the doctor gave her were really, really good.

"Your pop let me in, let me up here because I promised him I'd do right by you."

This hallucination needed to stop disturbing her sleep. "He'd never believe that."

"Thought that, too. Surprised the shit out of me when he said I could date you."

Jayde's eyes popped open again, she twisted her neck to stare at the man on her bed. "Date me?"

"Yeah."

"You asked my father if you could date me? Are you out of your fucking mind?" She pushed up onto her elbows and then moaned when a twinge of pain shot through her ribs.

Linc's jaw tightened and he frowned. She held out her hands and he assisted her to sit up against her headboard.

"I'm twenty-eight years old and you asked my father if you could date me like I'm sixteen?"

He released what sounded like an irritated sigh. "Baby..."

"And he said yes?"

"Like I said, trying to do right by you. Coulda forced my way in, caused a fight, more issues, more bad blood. Coulda took you home against his wishes. Didn't want to start our life together that way."

"Am I awake?"

His brows furrowed in confusion. "Yeah."

"Okay, then... Start our life?"

"Yeah. Gonna do it right this time. Gonna do it like we shoulda done it in the first fuckin' place."

"By dating me?"

He gave her a crooked smile. "Gonna earn his fuckin' respect. Jayde, want you to come home, but don't want you burning bridges to do so."

"Linc..."

"No, listen. Wasn't just about the baby. Shoulda told you that. I didn't. I fucked up with that, too. Shoulda told you how much that apartment felt like a real home with you and me in it. Together. Know it's a shit place and we'll get somethin' better, but wherever you are will be home no matter what."

Holy crap.

Before she could answer him, he continued. "Gotta tell you something, Jayde. Something I shoulda told you a while ago. Wanna make a life with you, so you gotta fuckin' know."

No way. Was he going to confess his love for her or something? Her heart began to race.

"Your pop probably told you most of it."

Nope, no declaration of undying love. But should she admit she already knew about his past or just let him tell her in his own words?

"But I wanna tell you the rest."

And she wanted to hear it. She reached out and grabbed his hand, pulling it into her lap. "Okay," she whispered.

"Was a jock in high school. Football. Wrestling. Was good on the mat. Did well. Made a fuckin' name for myself. Was being scouted by colleges. We're talkin' a full ride. Was bussed to one of the matches, then after we won, a bunch of us wanted to celebrate. Gettin' close to the end of the season and knew we were headed to States. Wanted to party. So jumped in a buddy's cage and did just that. Had a curfew, but my parents trusted me. Didn't rag on me if I was late 'cause not only was I good at sports, my grades were fuckin' good. By the time I could catch a ride home, it was real late... Like five hours past my curfew type of late."

He paused, his troubled gaze sliding away from her over to the window and he stared out of it for a few moments. She figured the best thing to do was to simply remain quiet and wait. She'd give him the time he needed to finish his story when he was ready.

He cleared his throat, turning his gaze to their clasped hands in her lap. His chest heaved with a breath, then he began again, avoiding her eyes.

"Tried to be quiet unlocking the door, trying not to disturb everyone sleeping, trying not to fuckin' get busted. My parents were cool, but they still had their limits. And that night I knew I pushed them. Walked in and it hit me like a fuckin' wall. The smell. Was overwhelming. Covered my face, rushed upstairs, found them... Found them all. Sleeping in their beds. Only not sleeping..." He paused, sucked in a ragged breath, then started again. "Almost thought about lying down in mine and going with them. Gas leak was so bad, figured it wouldn't take long. But something forced me back downstairs. Stumbled out the door and collapsed onto the grass, coughing, light-headed. Dialed 9-1-1. But knew it was too late. Everybody was gone... Everybody but me." He raised his green eyes to hers and she tried not to cry out at the suffering that he still so clearly felt. "I fucked up, Jayde. Me. I fucked up."

"No."

"Yes, baby, I fucked up. Took advantage of my parents' rules. Shoulda been home on time. Maybe coulda saved them. Got them all out."

No, how could he think that? "Or you could've died right along with them, Linc. That wasn't your fault."

"Yeah, baby, it was."

"Impossible."

"Later... *Fuck*... Later, found a voicemail on my phone. He left it at midnight. My pop asking where I was. Wasn't mad. Shoulda been. Shoulda told me to get my fuckin' ass home. Instead, his message said he hoped I was being smart and safe. Also said he and my mom were proud of me goin' to States, proud of how hard I worked to get where I was. And... And that they loved me."

His fingers twitched within hers and she gave them a squeeze.

She couldn't miss his Adam's apple rising and falling in his throat before he continued, "Last time I ever heard my pop's voice. Kept that phone. Still got that message. Should be a reminder not to fuck up, but I still do."

He was quiet as he stared at her, his gaze roaming over her face, which she knew was still swollen in spots, bruised and included a row of stitches over her one eye.

"Tired of fuckin' losing people I love, Jayde. Fuckin' tired of it. Lost our son. Can't lose you, too."

She opened her mouth, but nothing came out. Was he saying he loved her or just speaking in general terms? Just because he didn't want to lose her, didn't mean he loved her.

Did it?

Yes, that month they lived together in the apartment brought them closer together. How could it not? Those months of sharing the knowledge that they were becoming a family would tend to bond two people together.

Did she love Linc?

She stared at the man on her bed. The one who had convinced her stubborn father to actually let him in. An almost impossible task. But he'd achieved it.

"I named him."

"What?" Her chest became hollow, her breathing stopped. Her heart skipped a beat.

"I named him. Made him ours. Made him a reminder of how precious life is. How easily it can be lost. A reminder of how fuckin' hard I need to fight to keep you, Jayde."

"You named him," she whispered. She hadn't wanted to do that. Thought it would only make it worse by giving a name to a baby she'd never get to hold. That it would make their loss more real. More painful. "What did you name him?"

She watched in silence as he shrugged out of his cut and jerked his T-shirt over his head, tossing it onto the bed. She easily found the fresh tattoo amongst his myriad of others.

It was small. The letters in black script tucked between two other tattoos. But this one was close to his heart.

A reminder of what could have been.

"I spelled it that way for you."

"I..." She shook her head, then she dropped it into her hands as the tears began to fall once again. She thought she was done with crying. That she didn't have anything else left in her to give. But she was wrong.

Losing the baby gave Linc a chance to walk away. Why wasn't he taking that opportunity?

She sniffled. "Why are you here, Linc? Why? To make this whole thing even more painful than it already is?"

"No, came here to take you home. Promised your father I wouldn't do that right away. Told him I'd give you some time. But want you home, baby. Want you with me. So gonna give you two weeks. And every fuckin' day of those two weeks, my ass is gonna be standing on that porch, I'm gonna be knocking on that door and I'm gonna be respectful to your father, 'cause there's nothing more important than family, Jayde. Nothing. Jaymes made us a family and I'm not fuckin' letting that go."

She believed him when he said he wouldn't let go. His success in high school... Hell, his ability to get past her father alone proved what kind of drive the man had. When he wanted something, he worked for it and achieved it.

Only now he wanted her. She'd waited a long time for this. But... "Do I get a say in any of this or is it just you and my dad making the decisions for me?"

"Baby, anything you wanna say, say it. Gonna listen."

Jayde nodded and inhaled a deep breath, then let the words flow. "There's nothing I want more than to be with you. Nothing I want more than to live with you. And I want to do it because it's our choice and not because of a situation that forced us into those circumstances. I do want you, Linc. I do. I've wanted you for almost *five years*. I hoped you'd see just how much. But I feel like I forced you that night at Hawk's wedding. Forced you into being with me when I became pregnant. And I'm sorry for that."

He grabbed her hand and pressed his lips to her palm. "Jayde, wasn't gonna do what I didn't wanna do. Yeah, it surprised the fuck outta me, finding out I was gonna have a kid. Can't lie about that. But then, as I told you before, couldn't have happened with a better woman. Still believe that."

She thought about his words for a moment and then said to the man who could've walked away, but didn't, "I want to go home."

He closed his eyes, relief crossing his face as he whispered, "Oh thank fuck."

CHAPTER SIXTEEN

Two goddamn weeks he waited. Was nice as fucking pie. Respectful. Ate a little pride. All so Mitch wouldn't change his mind and decide Linc still wasn't good enough. Went every day to that middle-class house in the burbs, a reminder of where he grew up himself.

Every fucking day to spend time with Jayde.

Those were the two longest weeks of his life. He stayed at church every night, because he still couldn't bear to sleep at the apartment over the pawn shop without her.

Over those two weeks, he watched those bruises turn different shades and start to fade somewhat. But seeing her like that ripped his heart out every time.

Still sore, still in a little bit of pain—more on the inside than the outside—she was ready to get back to work. Ready to move in with Linc.

Then this morning when he went to pick her and her stuff up, Mitch had met him at the door. Fucking blocked it.

And Linc was ready to blow a fucking gasket.

He didn't want to cause a rift between her and her parents. He didn't want to be the reason she lost her family.

Or more like lost her father, really. April loved Linc. Axel had his moments. And fortunately, Z had given his presidential blessing. Though, with a word of warning about not breaking his baby sister's heart. Or sticking his dick elsewhere, where it didn't belong.

Fuck that. Jayde was the only woman he wanted to stick his dick into. Well, after she was finished recovering from the miscarriage. The doctor said to wait another month to be safe.

Another fucking month.

Linc blew out a breath. But as long as he had Jayde in his arms, he'd be able to wait. Just chock it up to anticipation. Hell, they'd waited over four years for the first time, four weeks... he should be able to do with one arm tied behind his back.

But right now he shouldn't be eyeballing Mitch Jamison—in uniform, no less—while thinking about having sex with his daughter.

Yeah, that was a bit fucking awkward.

"Two weeks isn't long enough."

"Gotta let go of her sometime," Linc muttered.

"I know you made an effort and, though I appreciate that, I'm still worried."

"As a good father should be," Linc said louder. He was hoping saying shit like that would butter up the stubborn fuck. But apparently, being a cop and a sort of *goody-two-shoes* biker made the man more stubborn than just being a plain ol' biker.

And bikers were stubborn as fuck.

So he figured he had to out-stubborn the king of stubborn. He just wasn't sure how.

But all those thoughts dissipated when Jayde pushed past her father with two large rolling suitcases in tow and stepped out onto the porch. "I'm ready."

Linc shook off his shock, unfroze himself from his spot and rushed forward to take them from her. "That all your shit?"

"Some clothes, other stuff. I'll get more later."

"Jayde," Mitch started, frowning at his daughter.

Jayde raised her palm up. "Dad, I know it's hard for you to believe, but I'm an adult now. I have a good job. I'm going back to school next month. I have a car, if you'll let me take it with me. We have a place of our very own, thanks to Ace. I can't live here forever."

"Yes, but—"

She lifted her palm higher and almost into his face. "Dad, your cop buddies complain when they can't get their adult children out of their house. You should look forward to an empty nest. It's time. You and mom need some alone time." She wiggled her eyebrows and her father rolled his eyes up to the porch ceiling. "Now you two can go hog wild." She smiled and patted his cheek. "Live a little."

"Jesus," Mitch muttered.

Linc dropped his head down and stared at the floor, trying not to release a snort of laughter at his woman's words.

"I'm only going to be a few miles away, Dad. I'm not leaving the country. Not even the state."

"Your education—"

"I'm already signed up for fall classes."

Mitch's jaw dropped. "How? I didn't receive the tuition bill."

"Yep, because we're paying for it. Or the club is. Either way, it's covered."

"Right. So you can be a criminal defense attorney," he grumbled.

Linc knew both Axel and Mitch had a problem with Jayde picking criminal defense as her specialty. Especially since she'd be trying to release the same people they put in jail.

"I want to defend innocent people. Whether they're falsely accused or are arrested due to shoddy police work. People like your son." Jayde shot her father a pointed look. "I don't want what happened to Zak to happen to others, Dad. He lost ten years of his life because of it." She stood on her tiptoes and pressed a kiss to her father's cheek, then held up a key fob. "Yes?"

Mitch's gaze bounced from the fob in her fingers to Jayde's face then to Linc before landing back on Jayde. After a long moment and an equally long sigh, he finally agreed. "Fine."

Jayde smiled and released a cute little squeal. "Thanks, Daddy. Love you."

Mitch closed his eyes and stood there silently.

Linc figured they'd better split while the splitting was good.

He yanked on the suitcase handles and rolled them noisily down the porch steps heading double-time over to her Camaro.

Jayde followed with a big smile and a spring in her step. He loaded up her car and waited until she pulled out of the driveway before following his woman home.

———————

Dinner. All of them at dinner. Since she was no longer on any pain medication, she couldn't blame the drugs, couldn't ignore that fact that this wasn't a hallucination.

Because it wasn't.

Linc's hand was on her knee under the table and every once in a while, he'd squeeze it. More like every time Mitch spoke, he'd squeeze it. She shot him a glance. Was he nervous sitting around the table with her family?

It started out awkward, which was no surprise, especially after the last time they tried this, when Z walked out.

But for whatever reason, Mitch—and, surprisingly, Zak—was willing to try again.

She wondered if her father banged his head during a police incident.

Z sat at one end of the table, disturbingly quiet. Their father sat at the other. And neither looked at each other.

That had to be awkward.

Her mom sat to Mitch's right, Axel sat to his left, then Bella. Sophie sat to Z's right, Linc to his left and Jayde was sitting in the middle across from Bella.

Axel was going on and on about something, but Jayde wasn't sure if anyone was paying attention.

Well, until he said, "And Ace wants to give her away."

Wait. What did she miss?

Axel turned his blue eyes to Z's end of the table. "Brother, want you and Soph there. It's important. And not just you. Bella's DAMC, so..." He sucked in a breath. "Shit. Don't know how this is going to work." He sat back and scrubbed a hand over his short hair. "I really don't know how this is going to work," he turned to Bella, "with both your family and members of the police department being there."

"Could be a fuckin' disaster," Z muttered.

"Maybe we should elope," Axel suggested.

"Maybe we shouldn't do it at all," Bella returned softly.

April leaned forward, saying, "You probably need to be married to adopt, Bella."

"Baby, we'll figure it out," Axel whispered to his fiancée.

"Right." Bella snorted. "I can imagine it now, a big brawl breaking out, D punching a cop and getting thrown in jail." She shook her head.

"You can do two celebrations," Jayde said. "One for us, and then one for the cops."

"Us?" Mitch asked, his gaze landed on her, then it slid over to Linc. "Us now?" He eyeballed Z. "He claim your sister at the table?"

Z pulled his shoulders back and pursed his lips, staring at their father before saying, "Yeah. Gotta problem with that?"

Jayde was surprised when Axel spoke up. "Dad, you knew that would happen. Shouldn't be a surprise."

Linc's fingers were no longer squeezing her knee, instead they had a death grip on her thigh. She slid her hand over his and squeezed gently. He released the grip, turned his hand over and intertwined their fingers.

"Dad, it's not like we're married..." *Yet.*

Color started creeping into her father's face. That was not a good sign. "I know! You're a biker's ol' lady! That's worse!"

"Here we fuckin' go again," Z muttered under his breath next to Linc.

"No. It isn't," Linc said. His head twisted toward Mitch to address him. "It isn't. Told you I was gonna do my best with your daughter. Claiming her is proof of that."

"Turning her into your *claimed* property is best for her?" her father blustered.

"Shows her how important she is to me. Shows my loyalty. My dedication. Sorry you don't see it like that, but that's what it is."

Mitch stared at her, his jaw tight. "Are you wearing his colors?"

"Dad—"

"Just on the club runs," Linc answered.

Mitch's nostrils flared. "See, honey? This is what happens when you become a man's property. You don't even get to finish your sentences."

April cleared her throat. "Honey, you do realize you do that all the time to me, right?"

Mitch turned to his wife and blinked.

Jayde rolled her lips under as her mother continued, "What's the difference between Andrew claiming Jayde at the table or sliding an engagement ring onto her finger? He's showing her how much he loves her."

Uh...

"It's true. Love your daughter. Gonna do right by her. Promised you that. Not breaking that promise."

Uh...

"An' he knows his ass is on the line if he does," Zak said to Linc with a raised brow.

Linc gave a nod to her oldest brother. "Got you, brother."

Zak gave him a return nod.

Hold up. They needed to get back to this "love" part. She couldn't let that go ignored.

Jayde leaned over and whispered to Linc. "You think if you're going to tell people you love me, you could actually tell me first?"

"Told you," he said under his breath.

"No."

His brows furrowed as he turned his full attention on her. "Yeah."

"When?"

"Mentioned it when you were still living here."

"When I was drugged up?"

Linc only frowned at her.

"Did I say it back?"

His frown deepened. Jayde glanced around the table to see everyone with their eyes and ears on them.

Shit.

"We'll talk about this later," she whispered.

Oh, but no. Her father wasn't letting that one go, either. "No, honey, let's hear it. You're wearing his cut. Living with him. Man tells you he loves you, I expect to hear an answer."

Jayde's jaw dropped as she stared at her father. The man was almost looking smug at the head of the table.

"Don't need to say it," Linc muttered next to her. "'Specially if it ain't true."

Wow. That... that cut her. "Linc..." she whispered.

"Can we get back to our wedding?" Axel asked.

Jayde appreciated the fact her brother was trying to pull the attention from her and Linc and that extremely uncomfortable moment.

But then both of her brothers were the bomb, which was cemented by Zak speaking up next.

"No, we can't. So no one dies, you're gonna need to elope, so that fuckin' conversation is over." Z said matter-of-factly. "Got somethin' else to talk 'bout. It's important. Figured might as well do it tonight."

Now what?

Everyone seemed to be sitting around the table on the edge of their seat. This time it wasn't because of awkwardness and nervousness. Now it was due to anticipation. Of course Z wasn't on the edge of his. He always sprawled in any chair—even an uncomfortable wooden one—like it was a La-Z-Boy recliner and managed to look cool about it.

Z turned toward his wife, who gave him a little nod, then he pointed his gaze at Axel. "Got a question for you, Ax. It'll affect Bella, too. Already talked to her an' she's good with it." Axel shot a glance at Bella, who ignored him as Z continued, "Askin' you two to take Zeke if anything ever happens to me an' Soph."

Axel's eyes became wide and he didn't even bother to hide his surprise. No, it was more than surprise. He was stunned, as were their parents. "Like his guardian?"

Wow. That was a huge step to fixing the remaining rift between her brothers. One she never thought would be smoothed over completely. And for Z to actually make that leap...

Zak lifted a shoulder and let it fall. "Yeah, like that. Even if somethin' just happens to me. Need you to step in an' be a father figure to my son. Know he's got the club to help raise 'im. Everyone would step in, help Sophie. Want 'im to grow up DAMC, got me? But, fuck, Ax... You're my brother. My actual blood."

Oh my God. Jayde peered into her water glass with suspicion. Had her mother drugged them all?

"Need you to step up if something happens, it's all I'm askin'. Willin' to do that for me?"

April slapped a hand onto Mitch and was squeezing his forearm so hard that her knuckles were turning white. Their parents' eyes met briefly, then they turned back to Axel, waiting for his answer. Jayde wondered if she appeared as shell-shocked as Axel did. His mouth hung open and it looked like he struggled to close it.

"I... Uh... You sure you want me and not Diesel? You two have always been as close as brothers." A look of regret slipped across his face. "Actually, closer."

"Yeah, but D's got his hands full already an' if you haven't heard, Jewelee's expectin' number two. An'..." He glanced at Sophie, who wore a secret smile, then back to Axel. "So's Soph."

April let out a high-pitched squeal that made everyone wince as she jumped to her feet, rushing over to Sophie and wrapping her arms around her. "That's great news!"

Jayde slammed back against her chair and blinked. She should feel happy, feel joyous like her mother, like Z and Sophie, who now wore huge grins. But she wasn't sure what she felt. Maybe a little bit...

Hollow.

She glanced over at Bella, but the woman showed no reaction to the news. While her face appeared neutral, Axel was watching her carefully. Most likely Zak gave her the heads up before announcing it to everyone else. But, what the hell, maybe he should have done the same with her and Linc. Especially so soon...

"Did you know?" Jayde asked Linc softly. She didn't think anyone heard her with how her mother was squealing and yelling and crying as she alternated hugging the stuffing out of both Sophie and Zak.

"No," was all Linc said, his face an unreadable mask.

But she was wrong, Z had heard her. He scraped a hand through his dark hair. "Fuck, sis, sorry. Shoulda warned you an' Bel—"

Their attention was drawn to Axel rising from his chair and stepping behind Bella to wrap her in his arms. She seemed to be fine until her brother did that, then she just looked sad.

"It's one thing I want to give you and can't," Bella whispered.

April became silent while they watched another shocking moment. Which was Mitch reaching out, grabbing one of Bella's hands and giving it a squeeze.

Who was that man?

Bella's words cut her deep. She knew how much Axel wanted a child with her. But that day would never come. It was one reason Jayde had gone to them about adopting her baby.

Their baby.

Jaymes.

Jayde wiped a stray tear from her cheek. Out of everyone at the table, she understood Bella's loss better than anyone.

She couldn't even be their surrogate by using one of her eggs, because the sperm would have to come from her brother.

So yeah. That wouldn't work. And Bella's sister, Ivy, had a hard time conceiving herself. Though now she would soon pop out Jag's first child. Otherwise she would have made a good surrogate.

"Baby," Linc murmured next to her, then caught another one of her rogue tears on his thumb. "You okay?"

She sniffled and nodded. No reason for tears, unless they were happy ones. Sophie being pregnant, giving Jayde another niece or nephew was good news, not sad. "Yes. I'm happy for them."

"Yeah," he breathed.

April moved around the table, giving Jayde's shoulder a squeeze before returning to her seat. "Well, now you definitely need a bigger place."

"Yeah. Movin' outta the bakery. Gonna build a place. DAMC's buyin' a big piece of property an' making a gated complex." He looked at Mitch. "Linc an' Jayde's gonna get a place built, too."

"We are?" Jayde whispered. "Did you know about *that*?"

Again, Linc answered with a soft, "No."

Z continued, ignoring Jayde's shock. "Yeah. Gotta keep family close. Keep 'em safe."

"That's quite an undertaking, Zakary," Mitch said quietly.

Z lifted his chin in the typical stubborn Jamison way. "Yep, sure is."

A cry came from the other room where Zeke was sleeping in a playpen. Before Sophie could push her chair back, Mitch was out of his. "I'll get him."

Jayde thought her jaw dropped for the millionth time that evening. Everyone just stared at Mitch as he left the dining room and headed into the den. Then they all just blinked at each other in stunned silence.

"Mom, are you drugging Dad or something?" Jayde asked.

April whispered, "I threatened to leave him if he didn't fix all of this."

"Mom!" Axel exclaimed.

"Holy shit," Jayde mumbled. "Mom laid down the law."

"Well, I'm tired of this division. It's gone on way too long. I shouldn't have to sneak around to see my own goddamn grandchild. Soon to be grandchildren. Having dinner at this table should be done every Sunday—"

"Club runs," Z muttered.

Their mother's light brown eyes landed on her oldest son. "What?"

"Runs are on Sunday, Mom. Party at church after."

Their mother waved a hand around in exasperation. "Whatever, I'll pick another night."

Z and Axel both groaned in unison.

"I work rotating shifts, Mom," Axel said. "It's hard to plan something weekly."

"Once a month?" she asked.

Jayde heard the hope in her mother's voice and didn't want to dash it. "Once a month would be great, Mom. Right, Linc?"

Green eyes blinked back at her. She jabbed him in the ribs with her elbow.

"Uh, yeah. Great."

Sophie leaned closer to Z. "You think your dad is doing okay with Zeke?"

Zak looked in the direction their father went. "Fuck," he muttered.

"I'm just saying, maybe you should go check on them," Sophie suggested. Jayde didn't miss the look in her eyes. The woman was a master manipulator—of the good kind—when it came to her husband. And apparently, the Jamison family in general.

"Fuck," Z muttered again.

"I can go check on them," April said, starting to stand.

"No!" Sophie yelled, then quickly recovered. "No, Zak can do it." She faced her husband. "Why don't you check, please?"

"Babe."

"Zak."

"Babe."

Sophie lifted her eyebrows and pursed her lips.

Z sighed, then muttered, "Fuck," one more time as he pushed away from the table.

Axel leaned forward and glanced down the table at Sophie. "You sure that's a good idea?"

"What's the worst that can happen? They get in a knock-down, drag-out brawl like you two did in the parking lot of The Iron Horse?"

Axel sat back and shut up. Bella was staring at the table, hiding a smile. At least she had pulled out of her funk.

"You did what?" April squeaked.

"Nothing," Axel muttered.

"You two boys got into a physical fight? And tried to hurt each other?" April's voice rose a few octaves.

Axel sighed.

"Axel, we'll get Kiki to draw up the emergency guardianship papers, if you're okay with it." Sophie to the rescue. Again.

"He's good with it," Bella answered.

"Um," Axel started.

"And have her include baby number two, as well," Bella added.

"Um." He glanced at Bella, then to Sophie. "Yeah, I'm good with it."

Bella smiled. Sophie smiled. April beamed. And Jayde figured it was time for her and Linc to get the hell out of there.

She had something important to tell him. And not at the table in front of her family.

CHAPTER SEVENTEEN

"It's been a month."

Linc glanced up from scrolling through his cell phone. He was sitting against the headboard and had been waiting for her to finish "getting ready for bed." Getting ready for bed for him meant stripping off his clothes, leaving them where they dropped onto the floor and then climbing into bed wearing nothing but his fucking tattoos.

For her. Not so much.

For her, it took what seemed like fucking hours. But then, the bathroom was stuffed full of shit he never saw before, never even knew existed. She had creams and lotions, gadgets and torture instruments for everything. And he really didn't fucking care what they were all for. He just knew it was like having a whole drugstore shoved into one tiny bathroom. Forget finding a spot for his razor and shaving cream. And in the shower... *fuck*... all he needed was a damn bar of soap. She had shit covering every available surface in there. Poufs, body washes, shampoo, conditioner, shaving cream... the shit was endless.

Women.

"Yeah," he said when he realized she was waiting for an answer.

She walked deeper into the room and stood at the foot of the bed. "I'm ready."

With zero makeup on her face and her long hair falling loosely around her shoulders... that alone was enough to give him a fucking hard-on. But her stating she was "ready" turned that erection into a ballistic missile. Especially since she was wrapped up in her silky pink robe that clung to her hips and clearly showed how hard her nipples were. *Fuck.*

"Yeah," he finally grunted.

"Are you?"

She normally just wore a tight little camisole that hugged her tits to bed along with some shorts that showed off her sweet thighs he couldn't wait to get back in between. But she never wore that robe around the apartment, so he wondered what she had up her sleeve.

"Yeah."

"So?"

"Baby, been ready. Just waitin' on you." He tipped his eyes down to the hard-to-miss tent in the sheet over his lap. "But wanna make sure you're ready."

"The truth? I've been trying not to jump your bones for the past couple weeks. I know the doctor said to wait, just to be sure, but... it was hard."

"It's fuckin' very hard," he agreed with a smirk, running his fingers over that tent.

Her lips twitched. "I meant the wait."

"Yeah, that, too."

"So, it's time," she said in the same way she announced that breakfast was ready.

"Coulda just climbed in bed and onto my lap. Coulda done without the whole production. Woulda got the hint."

Her eyes flashed, but her voice remained serious. "You think?"

"Pretty sure I woulda figured it out. Smart like that."

"I figured you just needed a bigger hint." With a wicked smile, she yanked at the tie and slid the robe off her shoulders. As it slipped to her feet, he sucked in a breath. He let his gaze roam over her *make-his-dick-hard* body. Her perky tits with their small dark pink nipples, her smooth skin, her stomach which was now almost flat again, the apex of her thighs with that small patch of dark hair. Her soft thighs that he wanted to sink his teeth into...

It was his body. She was his now.

His eyes flipped back up. *Wait.*

What the fuck was that?

There, a small tattoo on her left side at the top of her ribs. It was fresh, too. The skin was still red around the lettering. "What the fuck is that?"

She twisted a little at the waist to show him.

Holy fuck.

She had the exact same tattoo he had, but on her ribs. Small. Delicate.

Jaymes.

"I went to Crow this morning," she stated like it was a normal everyday occurrence.

What the fuck. And she didn't say dick to him about it until now? "Crow see you naked?"

Jayde rolled her eyes. "Seriously? That's all you can say?"

"Yeah. Had to take your shirt off for him to do that?"

"Yes, but—"

"Woman," he growled. He rolled up onto his knees, grabbed her arm and pulled her onto the bed with a jerk. Twisting his body, he rolled her underneath him. He planted his palms into the mattress on both sides of her head and stared down into her striking blue eyes.

He slowly rolled his hips to make her aware of just how hard he was for her. "Shoulda said something. I'da went with you."

"Why? Because you don't trust Crow?"

Fuck yeah, he trusted the brother, but he still didn't like the idea that Crow saw Jayde without a shirt on. The man was smooth. Way smoother than Linc. And he swore the DAMC women—hell, *all* women— had spontaneous orgasms around the ink slinger. "Really don't want another man seeing what's mine."

Jayde rolled her eyes. "He's a professional."

"*Riiiight.*"

"Speaking of *what's yours*, I really don't appreciate you telling me that you love me at my parents' dinner table."

"Babe, told you before. Just didn't listen."

She lifted one shoulder in a half shrug. "I'm not going to argue about it."

Thank fuck.

"Instead, I just want you to tell me again."

He cocked a brow. "Now? Gettin' ready to fuck for the first time in forever."

She pinned her lips together, and her eyes crinkled at the corners. "Not until I hear it."

"Told you."

"Tell me again," she whispered, and her soft voice swirled around his chest before heading south to land right in his dick. "Linc…"

"Yeah, baby?" he asked just as softly, lowering his head until his lips were barely above hers. He inhaled her warm breath and let it fill his lungs, then he gave it back. He rolled his hips slowly again, drawing his dick along the center line of her damp pussy.

He now knew for sure that he wanted to put another life inside her. To create a family with her. But he also knew now was not the time. She needed to concentrate on finishing law school. Achieve her goals. And he didn't want to hold her back. They had plenty of time to start a family. He needed to get them a permanent place first, anyway.

"Baby…"

"Yeah?" she breathed as their gazes locked.

"Love you."

Her body was warm and soft beneath him. Her pebbled nipples pressed into his chest. Her long, dark hair fanned out over his pillow, framing her beautiful face.

He had lost everyone he'd ever loved. So, yeah, it was hard to say the words, but she needed to hear them. She needed to know.

And, if he had to, he'd wait as long as needed to hear them from her. It would be worth the wait when he finally did.

She wiggled beneath him. "Fuck me. I've missed you inside me."

"Missed being inside you, too, baby."

"Show me how much you want me."

"Gonna do that," he said before closing the slight gap between their lips and taking her mouth. With another roll of his hips, he slid along her damp heat. She was ready for him.

And he was *oh-so-fucking* ready for her.

Even though he claimed her at the table a couple of weeks ago at church, he was now ready to claim her in his bed. *Their* bed.

It was time for a fresh start.

He moved down her body, sucking, licking, nipping as he went, pausing for a few moments on each nipple, pulling them into peaks with his lips, scraping the tips with his teeth, then he took his time sliding his lips over her belly. He paused and pressed his forehead lightly there, closing his eyes and just breathing until her fingers brushed over his hair. He thought about her tattoo, his tattoo, and the reason they'd finally ended up together.

If it wasn't for Jaymes, he might still be fighting this. What was between them.

If it wasn't for Jaymes, the Jamisons might still be a broken family. Hopefully, now Jayde's family could move on, fix the cracks no matter how deep they were.

Even if it didn't happen right away, they were on the right track.

And when Jayde finally gave birth to their first child, that child would have a family. Grandparents, aunts and uncles. Cousins. He or she would be surrounded by people who loved him.

And it wouldn't just be Jayde's family. It would be his. His brothers and their ol' ladies. Their kids. Their child would grow up in a huge, fiercely loyal family that looked out for each other.

What a lucky kid he or she was going to be.

"Linc," she murmured.

He inhaled a deep breath to clear his thoughts. He needed to focus on Jayde right now.

His ol' lady.

Hopefully his future wife.

Whenever she was ready.

He never understood why the other brothers wanted to get married. Zak, Hawk, Dawg. And he suspected Jag asked Ivy on the regular. The man would eventually convince her since he was relentless in his pursuit of her. Maybe after their baby was born she'd finally say yes.

Yeah, Linc hadn't understood the whole marriage thing since the women were already their ol' ladies. Which, for the most part, meant commitment.

But now he knew. While he liked that Jayde had agreed to become his ol' lady, had actually encouraged him to claim her at the table, told him she'd been waiting for a long time for that, he knew he wanted more. And having her wear his wedding ring, having her take his last name... Being able to call her his *wife*...

He wanted that. He needed that. His parents' marriage had been good. Great, even. He wanted and needed that, too.

So once she was done achieving her dream of getting her law degree, being a partner in Kiki's firm, if she wasn't wearing his ring by then, he'd make that his priority.

He trailed the tip of his tongue around her belly button, down through that little patch of hair, and he slipped it between her spread thighs, teasing her clit.

He pressed his fingers into her inner thighs and spread them wider, flicking her sensitive nub with his tongue, sucking it hard between his lips. Smiling against her as her hips jumped off the bed. Her moans and the fingers digging into his scalp only drove him to continue.

His woman tasted so good. Her scent of arousal only made his dick harder. But he wanted to take his time. It had been over six weeks since they'd had sex. Six. In the last four that she'd been home, in his bed, he'd made do with just wrapping her tightly in his arms, holding her close, breathing in the scent of hair, kissing her, touching her, but then stopping.

Sometimes, he'd finish himself off in the shower.

But now...

"Linc," she groaned.

He didn't answer her, only separated her plump, pink lips, sliding a finger and then his tongue through the slickness. Her feet were suddenly on his shoulders, her knees falling to the sides, her hips tilting to give him better access.

"Make me come," she murmured.

That had been his plan even though he was anxious to be inside her, to sink deep into her wet heat. To feel her muscles squeezing his dick tight as he slid in and out of her.

But right now, it was all about Jayde.

He wanted to show her how much he appreciated her. He did that by sucking her clit hard and sliding two fingers inside her.

The cry that filled the room was better than his favorite fucking song. Her little "yeses," "ohs," groans, whimpers, and gasps drove him out of his mind. The best was when she cried out his name.

Yeah, that he loved the most.

When her hips shot off the bed and her whole body went solid, he smiled against her pussy.

Fuck yeah, *he* did that to her. Him and no one else.

Nobody else would ever touch his woman again. Nobody but him.

Nobody else would feel that gush of wetness, her muscles clenching around their fingers. Their dick.

Fuck no. Just him.

"Linc..."

Yeah.

Just him.

He surged up and over her, pressing the head of his dick between her folds. He met her eyes. "Sure it's been long enough for those pills?"

They needed them to be effective this time, so he'd been making sure she took one every day. So she wouldn't forget to take one like last time, which was the reason, she eventually confessed, that she had gotten pregnant in the first place. While he knew she didn't do it on purpose all those months ago, he was there now to help ensure it was the perfect time for them both when she stopped taking them.

She nodded, her eyes unfocused, her face flushed. "Yes. *Please...*" Then she bit her bottom lip.

Her teeth sinking into her lip and her urging him with a groaned "please" was his undoing.

He wanted to surge forward, sink deep inside her. He closed his eyes and blew out a shaky breath. Because holding back was difficult.

"You don't have to be careful. I'm fine. Really."

He opened his eyes, met hers, and took her slowly. Her eyes quickly hooded, her lips parted and little puffs of warm breath escaped. Her neck bowed, and she released a long, low moan.

He began to thrust slowly while watching her face carefully. Brushing hair away from her forehead, he pressed his lips to her heated skin. He shifted enough to wrap one arm under her hips, lifting them higher, one arm around her shoulders, holding her close, then he gave her everything he'd been missing. What she'd been missing.

Hot. Slick. Tight.

Fuck.

He knew what she liked, so the more he rolled his hips, the louder she got. The louder she got, the deeper he rolled his hips.

He couldn't get enough of her sounds, the way her body reacted inside and out. And he lost himself for a while, letting those things circle him, sweep over him, take him under.

After a while, when he wasn't sure he could take anymore, wasn't sure he'd last much longer, he lifted his head to stare into those blue eyes of hers. The ones that got him in the gut every time. When she met his gaze, he thrust harder, faster, turning both of their breathing into shallow, ragged pants.

"Linc..." she breathed.

"Yeah, baby."

"Linc..."

"Yeah, baby, I got you. Just let go."

"Linc..."

Jesus. What was she doing to him? She needed to come before he did.

"I love you."

The little bit of breath left in his lungs rushed out.

Oh, thank fuck.

"Hang on, baby," he whispered into her ear. He pounded her as hard and deep as he could, grunting with each thrust and listening to her cries encompass him.

And when she came, it was like an explosion that swallowed him up and spit him back out. He drove deep one last time and stilled.

Only the sound of their ragged breathing filled the room. When she came she had dug her nails into the flesh of his back. That pain lessened as her fingers relaxed and her body melted back into the mattress.

He needed to get his weight off her, but he didn't want to move. He liked where he was.

No, he *loved* where he was.

He was where he belonged. She was where she belonged.

Jaymes might have brought them together.

But Linc would do whatever he needed to do to make sure they stayed that way.

CHAPTER EIGHTEEN

They'd done it. Axel and Bella went on a what was considered a "weddingmoon." Snuck off to an island resort without telling anyone and got married barefoot on a tropical beach. It was one way to avoid the conflict of trying to have a ceremony that included both sides of a very shaky fence.

One way to avoid having the Shadow Valley PD, the Blue Avengers MC, the Dirty Angels and the Dark Knights all at one location. Everyone recognized—and rightly so—that combination would be a disaster waiting to happen.

While it bummed out April and also, surprisingly, Ace, everyone agreed it was for the best.

And now Jayde sat under the pavilion at a picnic table watching her cop brother from across the courtyard at church. If a man could glow, Axel was currently doing so. He only had eyes for the love of his life and her for him. Nash's band had been playing slower songs for the past half hour so the newly wedded couple could hold each other tightly and move in a sort of slow dance/sensual grind around the grassy area in front of the stage.

While it was kind of sappy, seeing her brother so happy made her swipe a tear off her cheek.

Besides the Dark Knights, Axel was the only "outsider" at this celebratory pig roast. They had all gone on a long club run earlier in the day, Z inviting Axel and the Knights to ride along to kick off the celebration. It was a hell of a day.

She loved being on the back of Linc's sled. Whether her father wanted to admit it or not, she had been born for that spot. Born to hang onto her ol' man while the wind whipped at her face and hair. Born to feel carefree and happy with a powerful machine between her legs. And she didn't mean Linc, either. Though, she loved him between her thighs, too.

It was also amazing to see so many bikes in almost perfect formation as they rode through the Pennsylvania countryside, especially now that it was fall and the leaves were beginning to change. She could only imagine this was how her grandfather had been sent off by his club brothers after he'd been murdered. A run, a party, then storing the ashes in his Harley's fuel tank, which now sat in a revered spot on the mantel above the private club bar.

Even of more significance during the ride, Bella had worn her ol' man's Blue Avengers cut. The woman who had declared she was "property of no one" for so long and so loudly, had finally relented.

Diesel had scowled, grunted, swatted a huge hand her way, then stomped off muttering to himself when he saw that. He'd always vowed that Axel would never be invited on a DAMC run, but today was a new day, apparently.

Though, Jayde doubted her brother would ever be invited again. No, her brother and Bella would have to stick with the Blue Avengers MC runs in the future.

Ivy plopped down beside her with a sigh, her two-month old daughter in her arms. "Watching the two of them keeps making me cry. Nobody deserves happiness more than my sister."

"I know," Jayde murmured, her eyes glued to Alexis, the newest member of the Dougherty-Jamison family. Another addition that bound the two families in blood and not just brotherhood.

Jag had been beside himself when Lexi came into the world with a shock of red hair just like her mother. Her cousin had been absolutely thrilled because he said that if they were having a girl, he wanted her to look just like Ivy.

Jayde reached out and lightly brushed her fingers over that downy fire.

Ivy tilted her head as she regarded Jayde. "Want her? I could use a break."

Jayde could hear the exhaustion in her voice and even in the limited light, she could see it on her face. As she took the baby from Ivy, Kiki stepped under the pavilion to join them.

"Where's Ash?" Ivy asked her, as Hawk's wife settled herself at the table.

Kiki jerked her chin toward the clubhouse and shook her head with a snort. "Hawk's in there feeding him. Insists I pump so he can feed Ashton instead of me. Fucking D and Hawk. I don't know who's going to win the most overly-protective father of the year."

"D," both Ivy and Jayde said at the same time with a laugh.

"Probably right," Kiki grumbled. "It shouldn't be a damn competition."

Jayde cuddled a sleeping Lexi to her chest and a warmth swept through her.

Fuck. She knew that her and Linc needed to wait, but...

"Don't even think about it," came a gruff voice behind her.

"But—"

"Fuck no. Not now," Linc said as he came to stand in front of her. "Got school. Got work. When you're done with your degree."

"But—" Jayde tried again.

"Promised your pop to do right by you. Gonna stick to that."

"Linc's right, Jayde," Kiki said. "I need you to finish school and pass the bar. Hell, the club needs you to do it. It's too much for only me. Especially now that I'm buried in real estate crap because of this crazy neighborhood Z is building. I'm drowning in paperwork."

The first house—which was going to be Z and Sophie's—in this so-called gated DAMC "compound" was almost complete. The property was just outside of the town line but still close to church. Actually less than two miles. There had been a rabid rush of real estate negotiations and transactions when that property went up for sale. Z made sure that the club outbid all of the other potential buyers, even the ones with deep pockets who wanted it for commercial use. So it ended up costing the club a pretty penny.

Ace, the club's treasurer, said it was fine, the club was still in the black and the property was not only a financial investment but an investment in the future of the DAMC and the fourth generation... which was exploding.

The property was a hundred acres of fallow farmland and Kiki had made sure they had the option to buy the neighboring one hundred acres of woods next to it if it ever became available.

Diesel and Jewel's construction had just broken ground and there was a rush on that house since D's family was growing faster than he ever expected. Or wanted.

Jayde snorted when she thought of the reluctant father who was fiercely protective of his young like a momma Grizzly bear.

Even Axel and Bella were building a house on one of the lots so they could stop renting. Once they owned their own home, they planned on getting serious about adopting.

Z put Linc's name on one of the lots so once their home was built they could move out of the apartment above the pawn shop. But building a house was expensive and they had no idea how they were going to get enough money without them being indebted to the club. DAMC funds were already paying for her law degree. While her education was another investment Ace said was worthwhile, they didn't feel right asking Z to dig deeper so they could also have their own house.

Linc had been working longer hours at the bar so he could make more tips. He also was helping Slade and Diamond out at Shadow Valley Fitness part-time as a trainer to make some extra dough.

But he was working his fingers to the bone. When he'd finally fall into bed in the early hours of the morning, he'd sleep like the dead. And Jayde was worried about him.

Jewel came over carrying a red Solo cup.

"Are you drinking?" Jayde yelled in shock at her cousin. She had to be at least four months pregnant by now.

Jewel sighed and sat down, staring in to her cup. "I wish. I should be. That man..." She scrunched up her face. "Why did I ever get involved with him? Why did I choose the most hard-headed beast on the face of this planet? Why? Why would I want to be so frustrated on a daily basis?"

Ivy snorted and covered her mouth with her hand. Linc dropped his head and stared at his boots. Kiki just out and out laughed her head off before reminding Jewel, "The Eighth Wonder of the World."

"Oh yeah. But still... Can I have a do-over?" she asked no one in particular.

"No, woman, you fuckin' can't," came the low growl.

All eyes turned to D, who, of course, was carrying his daughter. Jayde swore they were going to meld into one person eventually. He held Vi out to Jewel.

Jayde's cousin planted one hand on her curved belly, shoved her other hand toward his face, palm out, and shook her dark head. "No. You don't get to pick and choose when you get Vi. You want her, then you keep her even if she takes a rancid shit. Got me?"

"Woman," D grumbled.

"No. Nope. No. There's breast milk in the fridge inside and diapers in the diaper bag. Deal with it yourself. I'm busy baking your other child right now and that's tough work since you produce monster babies." She groaned and stretched out her back. "If you don't start stepping up and doing the dirty work, too, then," she shook her head, "then..."

D cocked a menacing brow. "Then?"

Jewel sighed.

Ivy snickered. "She can't even hold out on sex with him."

Jewel frowned.

"Like I said, it's the ass," Kiki said with a chuckle.

"What's his ass got that mine don't?" Linc asked with an arched brow.

"Honey, you've got that special motion in the ocean with those hips of yours. Jewelee can keep that ass. I'll keep what you have."

"What the fuck," D muttered.

"If you're talking loosey-goosey hips, then *yessssss*," Sophie said as she approached. She was just beginning to show. "I've seen D's ass—"

"Who hasn't?" Ivy spouted.

Sophie continued, "And while it's spectacular, D. I do prefer Zak's—"

"No!" Jayde yelled, cutting Sophie off. "No. Noooo. That's my brother. Just no."

"Speaking of your husband, where is he?" Kiki asked.

Sophie waved a hand around in the air. "Chasing down Zeke. That kid is fast."

"Oh fuck. Is that Caitlin?" Ivy asked, her eyes narrowed as she stared toward the roaring bonfire in the middle of the courtyard.

"Yeah, and it looks like she's all over that hang-around," Jayde murmured.

Linc and D's heads both snapped in that direction.

"Where's Dawg?" Ivy asked.

"Apparently not watching his soon-to-be eighteen-year-old with raging hormones," Kiki mumbled.

"Baby," Jewel said.

"Fuck," D muttered. "Got it." He dumped Vi in Jewelee's lap and headed toward Dawg's extremely beautiful daughter and the *soon-to-be-removed-from-the-property-by-the-back-of-the-neck* hang-around.

"There's enough of us pregnant right now. We definitely don't need her to be added to that list," Sophie said. "Dawg would bust a blood vessel."

"He'd bust something," Ivy murmured.

Emma and Brooke joined them.

"Did you see your stepdaughter with that guy?" Ivy asked Emma.

Emma scanned the courtyard until she found Caitlin and D. "No. Does Dawson need to step in?"

"Got D on it," Jewel said.

Emma nodded and sighed. "Good. I know she's almost eighteen and I doubt she's a virgin... but..."

"But you and Dawg would rather not be grandparents before you have any kids of your own," Jayde finished for her.

"Yes. That would be preferable," Emma agreed.

"You'd better get started soon before Dawg does become Grand-Dawgie," Jewel laughed.

Emma didn't answer.

All eyes landed on her. Dawg's wife had her bottom lip caught between her teeth.

"Spill!" Ivy just about screamed.

"Well..." Emma murmured. "It's early yet."

All the women, including Jayde squealed at that news.

"On that note, gonna go check on The Iron Horse," Linc muttered. He pointed a finger at Jayde. "No ideas. You know the plan."

Jayde shot to her feet, careful of Lexi in her arms, and grabbed his face, pulling it down to her. With her lips just above his, she said, "Yes, we'll just keep practicing... for now." Then she gave him a quick kiss. He glanced down at the baby, smirked and swaggered off.

All eyes watched his departure, then the chatter began.

"Okay, so who isn't or hasn't been knocked up yet? Jesus. Raise your hand," Ivy asked. "Because I swear this club is going to double the population of Shadow Valley all on its own."

"Diamond," Kiki said.

That was true. Things between Diamond and Slade had been a bit rocky for a while after Slade found out the truth about what Pierce had done to her. Truth she never told him. But their rocking boat had seemed to upright and was heading once again toward smoother sailing. So everyone figured it wouldn't be long until she *was* pregnant.

"Brooke," Jayde said and all eyes swung toward Brooke, who had her lips pursed and she was staring out somewhere in the distance.

"Brooke," Kiki repeated.

"Brooke?" Jewel asked with narrowed eyes.

"Oh. My. God!" Ivy screamed, jumping to her feet. "Am I going to be an aunt?"

Brooke raised a palm. "We've decided to start trying. I had refused to drink the club water, for obvious reasons, but... now I am." She sighed. "While Dex is ready and raring to go, I'm a little apprehensive."

"Because of Dex?" Sophie asked.

Brooke shook her head. "Because of me. I just don't know if I'm ready. My business is booming and I'm crazy busy. If it happens, fine. If not, I'm okay with it. We still have plenty of time to start a family."

"It's definitely a lot of work and with running a busy business it makes it harder," Kiki agreed. "Luckily, Hawk is a good Mr. Mom."

Jayde giggled. "Who would have thought Diesel and Hawk would be good fathers?"

"How about simply fathers at all?" Sophie asked.

A murmur went through the women.

"We forgot Kelsea," Sophie said.

Brooke shook her head. "Let's hope that doesn't happen any time soon. She's a complete mess right now. I can hardly get her to show up for work. It's really bad and I'm concerned. I really want to fire her ass but Dex is worried that will only make her worse."

Another murmur went through them. Kelsea had gone on a downward spiral after finding out that Pierce was her father and her mother had kept that information from her her whole life. She had actually moved out of her mother's place and into an apartment with a friend. She didn't interact with the sisterhood anymore. She didn't show up at church. She hardly showed up at work at Brooke's interior design business.

"I love my sister," Brooke continued, sadness coloring her words, "but I don't know how to help her."

"It's just going to take time," Kiki murmured. "And we have to keep reminding her that we're all here for her if she needs us."

"Someone just needs to grab a hold of her and straighten her ass out," Ivy said.

"Crow," Sophie said.

"Mercy," Jewel suggested.

"Magnum," Ivy said, her eyes following the huge Dark Knights' Sergeant-at-Arms as he crossed the courtyard to meet up with Diesel, who had delivered an unhappy Caitlin to her father, Dawg. "Heard he kicked his ol' lady to the curb, for whatever reason."

Brooke sighed. "Whoever it is, is going to have a challenge on their hands. And those three wouldn't want to deal with someone who needs to grow the hell up."

"You never know," Sophie murmured.

"Okay, all this talk of babies and pregnancies and poor Kelsea... I need to go get a drink and find my ol' man," Jayde announced, handing a now-awake Lexi back to her mother. She pressed a light kiss to the baby's forehead. "Take care of my cuz."

Ivy smiled. "Anytime you want to babysit..."

Jayde laughed and headed back toward church.

L inc finished serving a beer to the customer at the end of the bar in The Iron Horse and then his gaze landed on Jayde who waited at the other end.

Hard to believe it was only months ago when she came into the bar to tell him she was pregnant. If he only knew then what he knew now...

He headed in her direction, only pausing long enough to make her a Captain and Coke, which was her favorite.

"You're not supposed to be in here working. We're supposed to be out there celebrating Axel and Bella's marriage."

He grunted and plunked the glass down in front of her.

She took a sip and winced. "Damn, that's strong."

"Yep."

"Trying to get me drunk so you can take advantage of me later?"

He cocked a brow at her. "Need to be drunk for that?"

She shot him a smile that went right to his dick. "No."

He nodded. "Didn't think so."

"But I don't want to fall off the back of your sled later because I'm all loopy."

He shrugged. "Hang on tighter."

"That simple."

He planted his palms onto the bar and leaned toward her until their faces were only inches apart. And like that night months ago, the night she scared the shit out of him with her news, he could see every shade of blue in her eyes. "Yeah, baby, you just gotta hang on tight."

She reached up and cupped his cheek, running a thumb over his bottom lip. "I am. I have no plans to loosen my hold."

He smiled, then snagged her thumb between his teeth for a second before letting it go. "If that hold gets shaky, I'll grab you. Make sure you don't fuckin' fall."

While her head was tipped down toward her drink, she was peering up at him through her dark eyelashes. "Mmm. Good to know."

He needed to take his woman home and take "advantage" of her. "Ain't gonna ever let you fuckin' fall, baby, promise you that."

"And that's why I love you."

Every time she said those three words to him... *Jesus*, it just got him in the gut. He needed to put a ring on her finger, he needed to build her that house. He was working on it but it was a slow go. She knew he was saving for the house; she didn't know about the wedding ring set he'd purchased.

He wanted that to be a complete surprise. He'd put it on layaway at a jewelry store in town and had a thank you to Jaymes inscribed on the inside of their wedding bands. Because even though they lost their son, he would be forever grateful for the gift their son gave them.

Which was each other.

EPILOGUE

Three years later...

L inc leaned back in the chair next to the hospital bed. He'd stripped himself of his T-shirt and cut and had his daughter laying on his chest. He wanted to be skin to skin with his newborn, to create that paternal bond with his baby.

Linc couldn't stop counting her perfect but tiny fingers and toes and staring at her perfectly pink, bowed lips as she slept.

His fingers stroked Adrianna's bare back in a constant soothing motion. She had her mother's dark hair and hopefully her baby blues would stay that way as she grew.

Linc's eyes rose from his daughter and landed on his cut where he'd hung it, then slid through the small, packed room. He might have lost one family, but he'd certainly gained another.

April was on the other side of the bed, talking softly with Jayde. The arrival of this grandchild was just as exciting to her as the rest.

Though Zeke wasn't in the room, Sophie and Z were there with their youngest son, Zane. Like Adrianna, the almost two-year-old was asleep against his father's chest, a string of drool clinging to Z's cut. Z gave Linc a chin lift and a grin.

Sophie was chatting quietly with Bella and Axel. Her stomach looked painfully huge. That was because she was carrying twins this time.

Only not Z's.

No, she wanted to bring the family closer together, so somehow convinced not only her husband, but also Axel and Bella to allow her to be their surrogate, using Axel's sperm but Bella's sister Ivy's eggs.

While it took some convincing for all of them, including Jag, to finally agree, eventually they did. And after two failed attempts, the invitro-fertilization finally took.

Linc swore Sophie was the Jamison family whisperer. She just knew what to do to patch the last of the cracks within the family. Unfortunately, her own family continued to shun her because of her decisions to be with the DAMC president.

Linc wished his own family could also be in the room, to see the perfect life he created with his wife and now his child.

But that loss, that hole that was left from losing them, from losing Jaymes, had been more than filled with not only Jayde's family but with his club, his brothers, their women, and their kids.

He still managed to fuck up but learned that sometimes those fuck ups made him stronger and appreciate what he did have all the more.

His gaze dropped to Jayde's hand on the bed, the one which held his wedding ring. He reached out, grabbed it, gave it a squeeze and then intertwined their fingers.

Jayde stared at their clasped hands before raising her gaze to Adrianna, then meeting her blue eyes with his. A soft smile spread over her face, then her teeth bit her lower lip and he knew she was trying not to cry.

Jesus. If she started, he might just join her. And, for fuck's sake, he'd rather not break the fuck down in front of everyone in that room.

Luckily, the door to the private room opening had him twisting his head in that direction instead.

Mitch, in full uniform, entered. His gaze swept the room before landing on his daughter. "Sorry I missed it." He moved closer to the bed, leaned over and pressed a kiss to his daughter's forehead.

"They find him?" Axel asked.

"Yes. Finally. Alive and well. He's now home with his family."

Axel gave his father a relieved nod.

Mitch missed his first granddaughter being born because of another child. One they thought had been kidnapped, but actually just wandered away and became lost. While he hadn't been scheduled to work, the man had volunteered to help search, even though he knew he might miss the birth.

Mitch's blue eyes flicked from Jayde in the bed to Linc, holding his newborn granddaughter. "How are things, son?"

Linc pressed his lips to Adrianna's dark silky hair. "Perfect."

Mitch's gaze bounced over everyone in the room once more, only hesitating for a few seconds on Linc's cut which hung off the corner of the bathroom door. "Damn near," the man said, his voice thick.

Right. Maybe not perfect.

But close enough.

Turn the page for a sneak peak of
Down & Dirty: Crow

Author's Note: *While the epilogue occurred 3 years later, Crow's book will start BEFORE the timing of this epilogue. I just wanted to give you a peek into the future of Linc and Jayde's life and also show you how the Jamisons were healing the breaks within their family. It was a slow process for them all, but they continue to move forward thanks to Sophie, Linc and Bella.*

DOWN & DIRTY: CROW

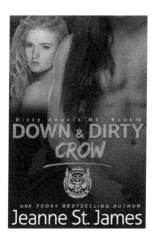

Normally I include the first chapter of the next book in the Down & Dirty: Dirty Angels MC series, which would be Crow's book.

HOWEVER, because there are spoilers on the first page of the book, I decided not to include it because I didn't want to spoil that book for anyone. Crow's book will be released March 9th 2019. On the next page I did include a little taste...

SNEAK PEAK OF DOWN & DIRTY: CROW

Chapter Seven

A buzz sounded and the heavy metal door in the small room on the other side of the thick glass opened and a heavily tattooed man in an orange jumpsuit, with his hands shackled to his waist, stepped inside. The same door slammed shut with a loud metallic clank and Rocky shuffled up to the window with shackled ankles.

He stared at Crow for a long minute, then took a seat, his bound hands in his lap.

"What the fuck you do now?" Crow asked him.

Rocky shrugged then grinned. "What I had to."

Crow sighed and sat back in his chair, crossing his arms over his chest. "You get the hole?"

"Yeah, for a couple nights. Was a nice fuckin' break." Rocky's salt and pepper head tilted and his grey-blue eyes narrowed on him. "Been a while, boy."

Crow grunted a "yeah."

"Have you seen my baby doll?"

"Yeah, I've seen her." Crow didn't tell him Diamond now lived next door to him. He wasn't sure Rocky would care and their time was limited. He needed to stay on point.

"Ain't knocked up yet?"

Shit. Rocky didn't know. Diamond hadn't told her father that she was pregnant. It wasn't his info to tell. "Don't think it's for a lack of tryin'."

Rocky sat back in his chair, his cuffed hands resting on his gut, as his eyes got a distant look. "Practice does make perfect. Sure miss pussy in here."

"Ruby must miss you, too," Crow said dryly.

Rocky's jaw became tight. "What I fuckin' meant—"

Crow cut him off. "Right."

Rocky's narrowed eyes were now focused on him. "Why you here?"

"Ready."

"For what?"

"Closure."

"Why now?"

"'Cause I need to learn to let shit go. That toxic shit that rots my gut deep down inside. Need to help someone else do the same. So need to be able to do it for myself first."

"Who? Isabella?"

"Bella's got Axel."

"Yeah, right. That nephew of mine would never step into this place to visit his murderer uncle. Don't want to get his fuckin' hands soiled. 'Kay, who then?"

"You never met her."

"Club property?"

Fuck. Was she? She was DAMC, so in Rocky's eyes... "Yeah."

"Who?"

GUTS & GLORY SERIES

COMING SOON!

Want to read more about Diesel's "Shadows?"

Keep an eye out in 2019 for the spin-off series starring the hard-core former special ops crew of
In the Shadows Security:

Mercy
Brick
Walker
Steel
Hunter
Ryder

And learn how they earned their call names.
More information coming soon!
www.jeannestjames.com

IF YOU ENJOYED THIS BOOK

Thank you for reading Down & Dirty: Linc. If you enjoyed Linc and Jayde's story, please consider leaving a review at your favorite retailer and/or Goodreads to let other readers know. Reviews are always appreciated and just a few words can help an independent author like me tremendously!

Want to read a sample of my work? Download a sampler book here: BookHip.com/MTQQKK

BEAR'S FAMILY TREE

		ZAK Jamison DAMC (President) b. 1985
	MITCH Jamison Blue Avengers MC b. 1967	**AXEL Jamison** Blue Avengers MC b.1987
BEAR Jamison DAMC Founder Murdered 1986		**JAYDE Jamison** b. 1993
	ROCKY Jamison DAMC b. 1964	**JEWEL Jamison** b. 1989
		DIAMOND Jamison b. 1988
		JAG Jamison DAMC (Road Captain) b. 1987

DOC'S FAMILY TREE

DOC Dougherty DAMC Founder b. 1943	**ACE Dougherty** DAMC (Treasurer) b. 1963	**DIESEL Dougherty** DAMC (Enforcer) b. 1985
		HAWK Dougherty DAMC (Vice President) b. 1987
	ALLIE Dougherty b. 1968	**DEX Dougherty** DAMC (Secretary) b 1986
		IVY Doughtery b. 1988
		ISABELLA McBride b. 1987
	ANNIE Dougherty b. 1971	**KELSEA Dougherty** b. 1991

ALSO BY JEANNE ST. JAMES

Made Maleen: A Modern Twist on a Fairy Tale

Damaged

Rip Cord: The Complete Trilogy

Brothers in Blue Series:

(Can be read as standalones)

Brothers in Blue: Max

Brothers in Blue: Marc

Brothers in Blue: Matt

Teddy: A Brothers in Blue Novelette

The Dare Ménage Series:

(Can be read as standalones)

Double Dare

Daring Proposal

Dare to Be Three

A Daring Desire

Dare to Surrender

The Obsessed Novellas:

(All the novellas in this series are standalones)

Forever Him

Only Him

Needing Him

Loving Her

Temping Him

Down & Dirty: Dirty Angels MC Series:

(Can be read as standalones)

Down & Dirty: Zak

Down & Dirty: Jag

Down & Dirty: Hawk

Down & Dirty: Diesel

Down & Dirty: Axel

Down & Dirty: Slade

Down & Dirty: Dawg

Down & Dirty: Dex

Down & Dirty: Linc

Down & Dirty: Crow

You can find information on all of Jeanne's books here:

http://www.jeannestjames.com/

AUDIO BOOKS BY JEANNE ST. JAMES

The following books are available in audio!

Down & Dirty: Zak (Dirty Angels MC, bk 1)

Down & Dirty: Jag (Dirty Angels MC, bk 2)

Down & Dirty: Hawk (Dirty Angels MC, bk 3)

Down & Dirty: Diesel (Dirty Angels MC, bk 4)

Down & Dirty: Axel (Dirty Angels MC, bk 5)

Forever Him (An Obsessed Novella)

Rip Cord: The Complete Trilogy

Damaged

Double Dare (The Dare Menage Series, bk 1)

Daring Proposal (The Dare Menage Series, bk 2)

Coming soon:

Dare to be Three (The Dare Menage Series, bk 3)

The Brothers in Blue Series

Down & Dirty: Slade (Dirty Angels MC, bk 6)

ABOUT THE AUTHOR

JEANNE ST. JAMES is a USA Today bestselling erotic romance author who loves an alpha male (or two). She was only thirteen when she started writing and her first paid published piece was an erotic story in Playgirl magazine. Her first erotic romance novel, Banged Up, was published in 2009. She is happily owned by farting French bulldogs. She writes M/F, M/M, and M/M/F ménages.

Want to read a sample of her work? Download a sampler book here: BookHip.com/MTQQKK

To keep up with her busy release schedule check her website at www.jeannestjames.com or sign up for her newsletter: http://www.jeannestjames.com/newslettersignup

www.jeannestjames.com
jeanne@jeannestjames.com

Blog: http://jeannestjames.blogspot.com
Newsletter: http://www.jeannestjames.com/newslettersignup
Jeanne's Down & Dirty Book Crew:
https://www.facebook.com/groups/JeannesReviewCrew/

facebook.com/JeanneStJamesAuthor

twitter.com/JeanneStJames

amazon.com/author/jeannestjames

instagram.com/JeanneStJames

bookbub.com/authors/jeanne-st-james

goodreads.com/JeanneStJames

pinterest.com/JeanneStJames

Get a FREE Erotic Romance Sampler Book

This book contains the first chapter of a variety of my books. This will give you a taste of the type of books I write and if you enjoy the first chapter, I hope you'll be interested in reading the rest of the book.

Each book I list in the sampler will include the description of the book, the genre, and the first chapter, along with links to find out more. I hope you find a book you will enjoy curling up with!

Get it here: BookHip.com/MTQQKK